D0815572

The Conjurers

Fight of the Fallen

Book Three

BRIAN ANDERSON

CROWN BOOKS FOR YOUNG READERS
NEW YORK

This is a work of fiction. Names, characters, places, and incidents either are the product of the author's imagination or are used fictitiously. Any resemblance to actual persons, living or dead, events, or locales is entirely coincidental.

Visit us on the Web! rhcbooks.com

Educators and librarians, for a variety of teaching tools, visit us at RHTeachersLibrarians.com

Library of Congress Cataloging-in-Publication Data is available upon request.
ISBN 978-0-553-49873-8 (hardcover)—ISBN 978-0-553-49875-2 (ebook)
The text of this book is set in 13-point Fournier.
The illustrations were created digitally.
Interior design by April Ward

Printed in the United States of America
10 9 8 7 6 5 4 3 2 1
First Edition

For Mom and Dad
Thanks for showing me what true magic is.

CHAPTER 1

ALEX

"Mom and Dad ran into a monster!" Alex swung around, facing his dripping crewmates—his sister, Emma; their friend Savachia; and Pimawa, their guardian and helper (who happened to be a giant rabbit known as a Jimjarian). "They sailed off to find the Eye, but they found this thing instead. Hideous, isn't it? They don't mention much else in the journals. . . . Whoa, you guys are soaked."

"Oh, really?" asked Savachia. He looked down at himself in mock surprise. "Thanks for the help, bookworm."

"I am helping. This is an expedition, not a pleasure cruise," said Alex. "Someone has to figure out where we're going. Look at this!" Alex held up the journal. "These markings match the ones I saw in the tunnel under the Tree of

AWEN

Dedi. You know, the one I had to go through to get to you, Emma, when you were battling all those . . ." He let his voice trail off at the look on Emma's face.

Emma slumped against the wall. "The tunnel that no longer exists because the Tree of Dedi *and* the Tower built on top of it collapsed? And nearly killed everybody we care about?" she asked sharply.

Alex knew she was angry at herself, not him. She'd been the one who'd led an army of Conjurians and Jimjarians into the massive Tower, built on what remained of the Tree of Dedi. She'd been convinced that the humans and rabbits could defeat the Shadow Conjurer. Instead, the Conjurer had disappeared, Emma's army had nearly been destroyed, and Emma herself had been turned into a Rag-O-Roc. Alex had used the Eye of Dedi, the most powerful magical object in existence, to turn Emma back into herself . . . but he had no clue how he'd done it.

Alex was aware that Emma had been tormenting herself for how things turned out. But even so, he was surprised by the words that came out of her mouth next.

"We should turn around," said Emma.

"What?" asked Alex. "No, Em. You're just scared."

"Of course I'm scared!" Emma shot back. "Pimawa said it himself. No one's ever returned from exploring the Sea of Dedi. That's where our parents went, and now they're gone! And look at what's happening to us! We're lost, we have no idea what direction we're headed, and we're going to sink!"

"We know where we're going." Alex held up the sea

chart. "Mom and Dad left us instructions in their old journal. They guided us to this chart. And we'll get where they went without sinking. Trust me. This is our destiny."

Emma raised her voice. "Our *destiny*?"

"Yeah!" Alex met her gaze. "We're going to be the ones who bring magic back to the Conjurian. Who find out the secret of the Eye of Dedi!"

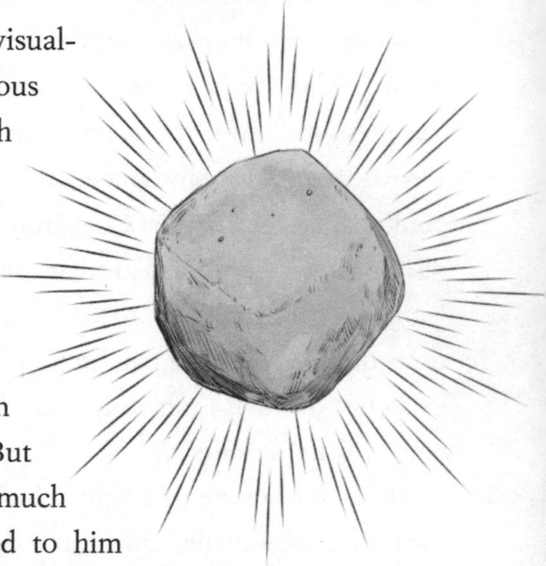

In his mind, Alex visualized the tiny, mysterious pebble that held so much power—if anyone could figure out the way to activate it again.

They'd left the Eye in Conjurian City with their old friend Derren Fallow for safekeeping. But Alex thought about it so much that it sometimes seemed to him that he could put his hand into his pocket and feel it there still.

Emma's impatient voice pulled him away from his memories. "Do you even care about finding Mom and Dad?" she demanded. "Or is this just about discovering the secret of the Eye? All our lives, you were the one who didn't want to tie his shoes without a plan. And here we are, in uncharted waters with—what? A few scribbles in a journal to guide us? And you think this is our *destiny*?"

Alex winced. "Of course I care about finding Mom and Dad. But you know I was just a baby when they disappeared.

I don't remember them the way you do. And you have to understand, Em, there's something larger at work here. Something bigger than all of us. Our way will be made clear. Trust me."

Emma rolled her eyes and didn't answer.

"Will the clear way include clear skies, Mr. Meteorologist?" Savachia wrung out his linen shirt.

"Listen, I was okay with all the touchy-feely talk about destiny while we were on dry land, but now we need everyone focused on keeping us above the water—literally."

"Let's stay levelheaded," said Pimawa. "I believe that Miss Emma is correct. I have one north worm left. It can help us get our bearings, and we can head back toward the harbor. The sea is too much for us."

The sea agreed, pitching the vessel one way, then the other.

"The ocean will always be too much for us," countered Alex. "That isn't going to change just because we head back to land. But our fate isn't going to let us drown."

"I doubt fate will plug the leaks when this carriage breaks apart." Savachia looked over at Emma, who was hugging one of the support posts. "We need to return to port temporarily and give it another go once the storms die down. What say you?"

Emma glanced around as if confirming the question was directed at her. "Um, yeah. Let's do that."

"Good," said Pimawa. "Let's get Gertie out of the water."

"What?" Alex looked from one crewmate to the other. "We can't just give up!"

"Actually, we can. It works for me." Savachia headed up the ladder. "Time for some fresh air. That includes you, bookworm."

Salty green water sloshed across the deck. Spiraling purple clouds crushed down from the sky, pelting Gertie with a hard rain. The mechanical alpaca paddled grimly ahead, towing the carriage through the waves.

Before leaving Gertie and the ship in Alex and Emma's care, the brothers Neil and Clive Grubian had done an exemplary job of making the carriage seaworthy. They had installed a large oval deck on top, with a railing of thick dark wood. A mast rose from the center, stretching five feet up like a curved pitchfork. A sturdy sail made from Myst fish scales hung between the two prongs. The ferocious winds strained the twisted ropes holding the fabric in place.

"We should douse the sail." Pimawa had the advantage on deck. Jimjarians were fishermen by nature, born with sea legs. Still, he made sure he had a handhold with every step he took toward the mast. "The wind will shred it!"

As Alex climbed out of the hatch, the ship pitched forward. He slid, hoping the gap beneath the railing wasn't wide enough for him to fit through. Inches before finding out, he jolted to a stop.

Alex rolled over, beaming up at Pimawa, who had a firm grip on his ankle. "I'm here to help," he said.

Pimawa clipped a rope to Alex's pants, tethering him to the mast. "Good. Start by turning that wheel counterclockwise." After pulling Alex to his feet, Pimawa took both of the boy's hands and placed them on an iron ring that had several wooden spokes sticking out. "Don't stop until the sail is all

the way down. Savachia, you and Emma get Gertie out of the water!"

"On my way!" Savachia raced past, arms out, skidding along the slick boards.

Taking a safer route, Emma pulled herself along the railing. By the time she'd made it to Savachia's side, her face was colorless.

Gertie was about forty feet from the boat. Emma grabbed the set of thick ropes that tethered the mechanical alpaca to the ship and heaved. The swells lifted the carriage so high, Emma lost sight of Gertie. Then the boat dropped. Emma gulped and kept pulling.

Pimawa lunged for the railing. "Keep turning that wheel, Alex!" He withdrew a glass test tube from his drenched vest. "The north worm has to see the horizon." Pimawa popped off the cork top. A yellow worm with black dots inched out of the tube. It looked around for a moment before shaking its head. "There's no way back to the harbor," yelled Pimawa, guiding the worm back into the tube. "He's not able to find north!"

Alex turned the wheel and grinned just a little, keeping his face down so the others wouldn't see. They thought he was an idiot, trusting in fate to get them where they were going . . . but look how it turned out when they tried to retreat. Fate wouldn't let it happen!

"Once we get Gertie secured," shouted Savachia, "we'll get below deck and wait it out!" He glanced at Emma, who looked ready to hurl at any second. Green-faced and grim, she kept pulling Gertie's line in anyway.

"The sail's down!" Alex announced.

Pimawa looked through the rain at the sail, securely bundled against the bottom of the mast. He smiled at Alex. "Excellent job! We'll make a sailor of you yet!"

Alex's eyes widened, but not in pride—in fear.

"Behind you!" he yelled.

Pimawa spun. Out from the foaming depths shot a large, semitransparent turquoise tentacle. It landed with a thud, wrapping itself around the railing and trapping Pimawa's arm. Pimawa pushed against the rail and tried pulling his paw free.

Alex released his grip on the wheel and yanked out one of the wooden pegs along its rim. He slid over to the railing and slammed the peg into the tentacle, barely missing Pimawa's paw. The slimy feeler went limp, dropping back into the sea.

Pimawa cradled his sore paw. "Thank you. That was quick thinking."

"Yeah." Alex gulped. "But I'm not sure I can think quick enough for *that*." Alex pointed at the swarm of tentacles twisting up over the railing.

"We need to get below deck," said Pimawa. "Emma! Savachia!"

Alex peered around for his friend and his sister.

EMMA

With a rope secured around his waist, Savachia hung over the side of the carriage, buckling Gertie onto a narrow platform designed as a dry dock for the alpaca.

Her back to Pimawa and Alex, Emma held the other end of the rope, bracing her legs against the spindles. "We're a bit busy right now!" she yelled to Pimawa. Why was he bellowing at her? Didn't he realize that she held Savachia's life in her hands? Ignoring the burning sensation shooting through her arms into her spine, she held tight.

As she stared into the turbulent water, she almost thought she saw the Shadow Conjurer's scarred face there, surrounded by all the Jimjarians and Conjurians who had blindly followed her into battle. She'd convinced them that fighting was the right thing to do. She'd told them that they had a chance, an actual chance, to win. And then . . .

The rope slipped. No! Emma shook her head. She wouldn't fail Savachia. Pulling hard, she reset her legs and ground her teeth, fighting back against the pain. The Shadow Conjurer's face dissolved, replaced by a mountainous wave, fifty feet high, rolling toward the carriage.

"Savachia! Hurry!" Emma yelped. Then over her shoulder she shouted, "Brace for impact!"

The rogue wave thundered forward, blotting out the sky. The rope in Emma's hands went slack.

She nearly fell backward onto the slick, wet deck but recovered and lunged for the railing. Savachia! Where was he? Had he fallen? Had he drowned? Emma gripped the railing and leaned perilously far over it, peering into the pelting rain.

A hand grabbed the railing next to hers, and Savachia swung over it. He caught Emma's shoulder and pulled her back.

"Trying to ditch me again?" said Savachia.

With a word, Emma pointed up at the wave cresting above them.

"I hate this ocean." Savachia sighed. He grabbed a rope coiled by Emma's feet and hurriedly lashed them both to the railing. "Hold on tight!"

The ship pitched straight up the front of the wave. Emma watched the crest crumble down in a frothing mass of destructive power. The wave swallowed them up, smashing the helpless carriage.

CHAPTER 2

EMMA

Gertie clicked gratefully as Emma unbolted her harness. Farther down the beach, Pimawa flopped next to a trunk. Wiping wet sand from his fur, he glanced around at the supplies they had dragged from the wrecked carriage. "I think that's all we can salvage."

Still equipped with her paddle legs, Gertie flippered toward Pimawa. Emma guided her along until the mechanical alpaca crumpled onto the sand, resting her head against a sack of flour.

"Oh my." Alex had been sitting next to the sack that Gertie had just chosen for a pillow. Now he sat up slowly, turned his head from side to side, and froze. "This—this is it."

Emma sat down too and rolled her eyes. She didn't need Alex to give her a lecture about how meager their supplies were. "How long will these last us?" she asked, ignoring her brother as he broke into a flurry of activity.

"If we're frugal, about a month," Pimawa answered. "That includes the secret stash of whistleberries, dried sponge nuts, and jelly I found. Bless those Grubians."

"Alex, do you think a month will be enough time to fix the carriage?" asked Emma. No answer. She leaned over the sack, watching her brother pick through the supplies. "What are you doing?"

"I need some stuff," Alex answered her. "I've got to—Whoa!" He held up what looked like leather bracelets with metal tubes attached. He flicked the tiny lever attached to one of the tubes. Sparks flared from inside it. "Cool. Pim, what are these?"

"Careful!" Pimawa answered. "Those make fireballs. You're lucky they weren't loaded with flash paper."

"You mean this?" Alex held up what appeared to be a small notebook sealed in a plastic bag. "We won't have any trouble getting a fire started." He placed a bracelet in his pack before buckling it closed, and then he tested the bag's weight before slinging it over his shoulder. Zeroing in on a section of broken railing, Alex seized hold of the wood and planted one end into the sand, leaning on it. It bowed a little. Satisfied, he yanked it out of the sand and jabbed the jagged end in the air a few times.

Emma rolled her eyes. Her younger brother tended to get distracted if she didn't keep him focused. "Alex, come on. I asked you a question. Is a month long enough for you to repair the carriage— Hey!" Alex had started marching across the beach toward the jungle. "Where are you going?"

"Exploring," said Alex, as if it should have been obvious.

"Exploring?" Emma threw up her hands in exasperation. "We've got to fix the carriage!"

Alex kept walking. "Mom and Dad *knew* this place," he said.

"Huh? Wait, stop!" shouted Emma. "We're all staying right here until we figure out how we're getting off this island."

Her brother paused, turning to her. "Emma, I know you don't want anyone else to get hurt. But don't worry. This is *my* call. You're not responsible."

The words stung. Emma thumped her head against the sack. Just a little over a month had passed since she had almost led her friends and half the Conjurians to their deaths—and now she was supposed to stand idly by and let her brother head off into the jungle alone? No way. Not going to happen.

"Emma's right, Alex," said Savachia. "It's not smart to go running off."

"We're lucky to be alive," Pimawa added. "We don't need to tempt fate."

"Lucky?" Alex planted his impromptu walking stick in the sand. "We survived a hurricane, escaped from sea monsters, and washed ashore on what is probably the only chunk of land within a thousand miles, and you think that's *luck*? You know what the odds of that happening are? This didn't just happen by chance. We were *supposed* to end up here. This is the exact island Mom and Dad described in their notes. I knew it the minute I looked around."

Emma listened to the arguing and felt helplessness wash through her. She knew that look in Alex's eyes perfectly well. He wasn't listening to a word anybody said.

"We don't know this is *that* island," said Pimawa.

"It is," Alex insisted. "I know it is. Fate brought us here."

Savachia studied the primal forest. "Would've been nice if fate had just booked us on a cruise instead."

"Make all the jokes you want," said Alex. "Pim, you're

the one always going on about how this sea has swallowed every explorer who ever set sail. But not us. We survived for a reason."

"We haven't survived yet," said Savachia. "We should hang here. Come up with a plan."

"Great, you do that." Alex kept walking, and Emma knew the only way to stop him would be to tackle him. "If I find any marshmallows, I'll bring them back in time for ghost stories around the campfire," Alex called over his shoulder. He trod into the thick foliage, batting aside leaves larger than his body and swatting at some unseen bug.

Emma watched her little brother walk away. She couldn't stop him. She couldn't do a thing. Useless. She was useless.

Pimawa and Savachia exchanged uncomfortable glances. "As a precautionary measure," said Pimawa, "I will join Alex on his nature hike."

Emma didn't budge.

"Right, off I go," said Pimawa, standing up. "If I may be presumptuous, you two can set up camp. Shelter, fire, and such."

"Take this." Savachia dug into the pile of rescued goods and pulled out what looked like a small trumpet with a trigger. He tossed it to Pimawa.

"A flare gun?" Pimawa held the device gingerly by two fingers.

"Just in case," said Savachia. "You probably won't need it but—"

"Yes." Pimawa eyed the dark jungle. "Just in case." He

tucked the gun into his waistcoat and hurried off after Alex.

"You should go too," Emma muttered. Savachia had never been one to turn down adventure.

"Nah." Savachia watched as the Jimjarian disappeared into the enormous fern leaves. "We should get started on a shelter. Let's see where our smuggler friends packed the tents."

Emma brushed sand off her pants. "Please. Go after them. I'm sure Alex's bravado will falter after he sees the first snake, and who knows what else lives in there. You'll take care of him."

"You'd be all alone. Who would take care of you?"

Emma balled her fists. She was no coward. They were all acting like she needed a babysitter.

Savachia eyed her, and he looked as if he'd decided that he feared her wrath more than he feared for her safety. "I'll go," he said quickly. "You're right—who knows what lives on this island. And your brother's head is a little full of loopy-loo hand-of-destiny garbage." He picked through the supplies, slid a rusty machete into his belt, threw aside a pair of rotted boots, took out a hard, domed hat, and put it on.

"Be careful," said Emma.

"That's no fun," said Savachia. "I'll come back. With both of them. Might want to get a jump on finding those tents. Looks like a storm's heading this way."

Emma watched the purple-and-blue clouds spreading out over the distant horizon. When she turned again, Savachia was already at the tree line, whacking the leaves with his machete.

"Away, you foul beasts!" yelled Savachia. "I, Sir Sheridan, plant slayer, command thee!"

Emma couldn't help a tiny smile.

Slowly the sound of the machete whacking at the foliage and Savachia's wild cries for the unconditional surrender of all plant life faded.

They'd be back soon. Of course they would, she told herself, and she turned her attention to the pile of rations, determined to have camp set up before the others returned.

They'd stay here on the island until the carriage was all fixed up. Then they'd sail back to Conjurian City for more supplies. They'd wait until it was safer and try again. That wasn't cowardice; that was reasonable thinking.

It took time, but soon enough, Emma had two tents staked on the sand. She was plastered with sweat when the first clash of thunder boomed close by. Too close.

A ball of twinkling light caught Emma's eye. The streak arched over the jungle like a baby comet.

The flare gun!

Her first thought was that the gun had gone off accidentally. Pimawa had probably caught up with Alex, and Alex had wanted to check the gun out and set it off. That would be like him.

Then Emma heard Alex's scream. Emma wanted to race into the trees to help her brother. To help her friends. But her legs weren't moving. Why weren't her legs moving?

She knew why. The last time she had rushed into a fight, it had ended in disaster. But this wasn't then, this was now, she told herself. Alex needed her. Pimawa and Savachia needed her.

Squeezing every last reserve of willpower, Emma took several heavy steps toward the jungle. Then she stopped. She couldn't. Just couldn't do it.

Another distant cry, and all of a sudden she was moving, each step stiff as though her legs were numb, frostbitten to the bone.

A flock of winged creatures took flight after another chorus of screeches, as if the jungle had come to life, directing its anger at the trespassers.

Finally, Emma ran, not knowing what she would find.

CHAPTER 3

EMMA

The plants cut Emma's skin. Alien sounds came from all around. Winded, dizzy, lungs burning, she struggled across the dense terrain. Alex should've listened to her. They all should have listened to her. They should've stayed on the beach!

The branches and vines slapped relentlessly at her face, defending the jungle against another unwanted visitor. She spat out a chunk of leaf. A thick vine clotheslined her in the stomach, flipping her headfirst down a slope of slick undergrowth. Her feet found the ground, and she stumbled into a clearing and promptly fell facedown on a bed of crunchy dead leaves.

Bracing herself up on her elbows, Emma brushed leafy

bits from her face. All around her, jagged walls of stone rose from the ground like rotted teeth covered in vines.

"Emma, get my machete!"

Emma rolled over and stared up into the air. A net swayed above her. Savachia, Alex, and Pimawa were squished inside.

"My machete, Emma!" Savachia called, wriggling his only free hand through the webbing.

Emma got to her hands and knees. She scoured the layers of dead plants.

"Hurry, Em," said Alex.

A crunching noise from her left halted her search. There was nothing there, at least nothing she could see.

Another noise rustled from the right. Someone or something was hiding just beyond the ruins.

Now the noises came from every direction. Emma twisted her head, catching glimpses of swaying leaves here, a few leaves settling to the ground there. She doubled her frantic efforts, running her hands through the ground cover.

Then the chittering started. Whatever creatures were circling the clearing, they were communicating. She closed them out, focusing only on finding the machete.

Her knee hit something hard. She groped under the leaves, hoping she didn't grab the sharp end. Bingo! Shaking, she stood, holding the machete out. Slowly she turned in place, wondering from which direction the first attack would come.

"Cut us out!" yelled Savachia.

"Oh, right!" In her panic about the noises, Emma had almost forgotten what she'd actually wanted the machete for. She stretched her free hand up until she could grab hold of the net. Then she lifted herself off the ground, bringing the machete up and carefully threading it between the webbing, hoping she didn't slice into Savachia.

The blade was dull. She sawed away.

"Hurry!" said Alex.

"What do you think I'm doing?" snapped Emma. "This netting is tough."

She kept sawing, listening to the rustling grow closer and closer.

"What's out there?" asked Emma.

"No idea," said Savachia. "Hurry up so we don't have to find—"

The first bit of webbing snapped, and suddenly strands were giving way in every direction. All three captives fell out of the net onto Emma.

"Get off!" yelled Emma.

"Sorry!" Alex rolled off the pile of bodies, then helped Pimawa up.

Savachia, who had fallen across Emma's chest, made no effort to move.

"Savachia!" said Emma. "Oh, for—" She twisted sideways, rolling Savachia over. And she stared at the expanding red stain on his shirt.

Emma looked at the glistening machete in her hand. "Oh no, no, no! Alex! Pimawa! Help!"

Pimawa leaped to Savachia's side, while Alex just stood there, massaging his neck. "Em, he's going to be okay."

"He's been stabbed!" Emma carefully lifted Savachia's head onto her lap. He stared blankly up at her. Was he in shock? "I stabbed him!"

Pimawa had already pulled his own shirt off. He leaned in and unbuttoned Savachia's. "We'll get a quick bandage on it and get him back to the beach. We can't stay here."

Emma checked the surroundings. Silent. "I think they're gone. Whatever they were."

"Good," said Pimawa, wrapping his shirt tightly around Savachia's wound. "Savachia, do you think you can walk?"

"I—I—uh, yeah," Savachia mumbled. "Don't think it's

too bad. Pretty sure if Emma had meant to kill me, I'd be dead."

"It's not funny," said Emma.

"Sure it is," Savachia told her. Pimawa leaned over the boy, who slung an arm around the Jimjarian's shoulders. Pimawa pulled him upright.

"Emma, come on," Savachia wheezed. "Not your fault. Who doesn't stab someone when they fall on them?"

"Let us be on our way," said Pimawa. "Before our captors return."

"Great." Alex retrieved his satchel. He shook off the debris. "There's kind of a path over here. I'll check it out and meet you guys back at the carriage."

"You can't be serious!" Emma gasped. "You nearly got us all killed. Now you want to go wandering off again?"

"I didn't ask everyone to come with me," said Alex, looking nettled. "Besides, we're fine. Uh . . ." He winced at the sight of Savachia's bloody shirt. "Some of us more than others. Look, we are meant to be here. We are meant to find out what secret this island is holding. And we can't do that sunning ourselves on a beach." He started off, following the path toward a gap between two crumbling walls.

"Get over here!" yelled Emma.

"Emma," said Pimawa, straining under Savachia's weight. "I'm afraid we must get Savachia to the carriage. We risk infection the longer his wound is untreated. Please."

"Alex!" Emma called again. But she felt her voice weaken. She knew her brother wouldn't listen to her, and he was already out of sight.

Savachia let out a soft moan and slumped against Pimawa's side.

"We have to get him out of here," the Jimjarian insisted. "And I need your help. We'll come back for your brother."

"But . . ." Emma felt as if the clearing was spinning. She struggled for breath. "We can't . . . I don't . . ."

Then Alex let out a loud yell.

"He's in trouble!" Emma charged forward but stopped as Alex exploded back into the clearing along the same path he'd taken a minute before.

"They're coming!" Alex bellowed. He barreled into Emma and grabbed her arm. Behind him, the jungle erupted.

In less than a minute, a surging mass of small, hairless creatures, smaller than newborn babies, surrounded them. Naked save for a few blue leaves strung around their waists, they circled their captives. A few darted forward and then dodged back, snarling with thorny teeth.

Emma wished she had held on to the machete. She wished she had never entered the jungle. She wished their whole lives didn't constantly feel like a bad dream!

“Sounds like the tea is ready, Pim,” Savachia mumbled. He sagged closer to the ground.

“He’s going into shock,” said Alex calmly, as if he weren’t even worried about the beasts nipping inches from his legs.

“Imps,” sighed Pimawa. “Why couldn’t it have been snakes?”

“What do we do?” asked Emma.

“I’m not sure.” Pimawa dragged Savachia closer, away from an imp who clawed at his shoe. “These aren’t domesticated imps. They’re feral.”

“I say we stomp a path through them,” said Alex. “They’re a nuisance and slowing us down.”

“Not the best idea,” said Pimawa. “They’ll strip you

down to a skeleton in seconds." He jerked Savachia's feet
second time.

"This is completely ridiculous!" Alex knelt, digging i
his pack. "It's not at all why we are here." He withdre
tiny pouch, loosening the drawstrings. "Okay, huddle up
cover your eyes."

Realizing what her brother was doing, Emma slappe
hand over her face and the other over Savachia's.

"Happy Not-Going-to-Eat-Us Day!" Alex sh
Twirling in a tight circle, he scattered the contents
pouch over the encroaching imps.

The imp's bulbous gray eyes widened as glitt
sparkled, flared, and ignited in a flash of green-ar
flames. A collective squeal went up from the imps

scrambled over themselves to get away from the flames. Then they were gone.

Emma stared. "Did they just . . . leave?" she asked.

"No," Pimawa answered, pointing to the moving leaves at their feet.

"Whoa, they're invisible," Emma whispered.

"Yes. It's a trait that made them attractive as assistants back in the early days of magic," said Pimawa. "However, domestication was a failure, given their taste for human flesh."

Emma glared at Alex. He'd only made things worse. "What do we do now?" she asked.

"Walk very slowly," Pimawa advised. "And, Emma, please help me. Savachia is too tall for me to carry alone."

"Come on, Alex!" Emma ordered. She slipped her shoulder under Savachia's free arm, but before she could grab hold, Savachia was torn from her grip.

With a scrap of Savachia's shirt in her hand, Emma watched helplessly as the boy, now barely conscious, appeared to float back into the ruins. The earth below his body churned from hundreds of small, invisible feet.

Diving after him, she managed to grab hold of Savachia's shoe. It popped off his foot, leaving her facedown on the ground—again.

She got to her hands and knees, her heart thudding in her chest. Those things—those horrible little imps—were going to eat Savachia! She had to do something—

Then Savachia's limp body hit the muddy earth with a thud. He lay there, helpless, as the undergrowth in all directions thrashed as in a whirlwind. Dozens of unseen bodies were fleeing into the jungle.

As soon as they'd come, the imps were gone.

ALEX

Alex slid to a stop next to his sister. He looked at Savachia in puzzlement. "But why would those imps leave their meal behind? They didn't want to a moment ago. There has to be"—his eyes flashed in horror—"something else."

The jungle shook. Vines snapped. Limbs tore from trunks. Something big was coming right for them. Moving fast.

Pimawa hurried forward, grabbing the machete. He held it out in front of him as steady as he could.

"We won't be able to outrun whatever it is," said Pimawa. "We have to fight."

The jungle roared. Alex stared as the nightmare from his parents' journal bounded toward them. It was Awen. Awen the Immortal.

The drawing had been scary enough. The real thing was much worse. As big as the trees that surrounded it, Awen advanced step by thundering step. It looked a lot like a tree, in fact, Alex thought as he gawked. Two skinny limbs, very much like branches, flailed out from a body like a trunk. A face made of wrinkles and whorls of bark snarled as the thing lurched forward.

Alex knew that fate had led them here. But he was starting to wonder if fate wanted them all dead.

CHAPTER 4

DERREN

Early morning sun glinted off the polished bone-white hood of the antique sports car. Traffic thickened as Derren Fallow drove through the Las Vegas strip.

Next to Derren, on the maroon leather passenger seat, a green parrot stirred. The bird stretched his wings, yawning, and retrieved his sunglasses from the glove box.

"Check it out." Derren nodded at a billboard.

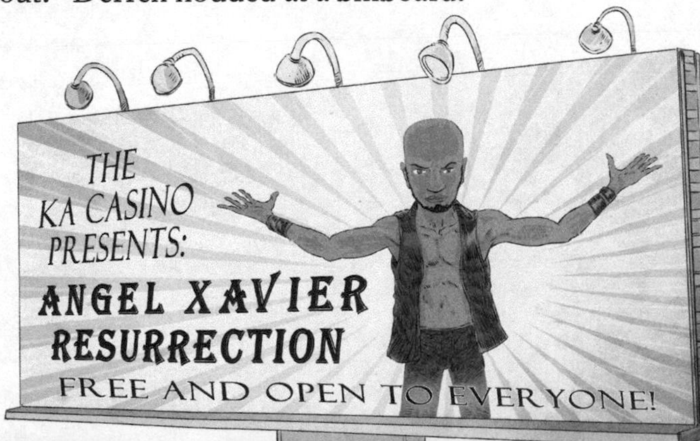

"I must say," squawked Geller. "After what you did to him in that cave, it is going to be a truly dull show."

Derren ignored Geller's joke. "It would seem our host has something planned. She must know Xavier is dead, and yet . . . Makes me nervous, Geller. Working with non-magicians always does. At least with magicians, I know their tricks."

Ahead, outlined in the rising sun, was a pyramid, dwarfing the neighboring buildings—the Ka Casino. Derren parked and tossed his keys to a valet, and then headed straight into the entrance.

Next to the door was a sign.

Derren shook his head as he strolled by.

The lobby of the Ka Casino replicated an Egyptian tomb, complete with an oversized sarcophagus. Derren ignored tourists on every side as he headed down a hallway.

A twelve-foot-tall, cat-headed statue sat abandoned against the back wall. Derren fished a badge out of his pocket and waved it at the statue's head. A door hidden on the side of the sandstone sculpture slid open, and Derren stepped inside. His stomach flew upward as the elevator dropped with barely a hum.

It had been some time since Derren's last visit with Latiff. Six years, to be exact. It was then that they'd come up with the idea of Sanctum—a secret cabal of scientists bent on using science to unlock the secrets of magic. And that's where they'd conceived the Shadow Conjurer together.

But while Derren had been busy using the Shadow Conjurer to gain control of the Conjurian, Latiff had built the Ka Casino, a cover for Sanctum's operations. Now Derren was beginning to get the idea that Latiff was up to much more than she'd ever told him.

And she was still running that contest to find a psychic who could actually contact the dead? He'd thought she'd be over that by now.

The elevator stopped with a soft thud. The door slid open, revealing a broad woman in the black uniform of Sanctum. She had short, spiked red hair and an even spikier expression. Two more guards flanked her.

"Mr. Fallow," said the guard. "This way, please."

The two guards moved to either side of Derren. Each had a small, thick baton, which Derren knew could deliver an unpleasant electric shock. "And you are?" Derren asked, eyeing the woman in front of him.

"In charge," replied the spiky-haired guard. "I am Captain Blaine, head of Sanctum security. This way, now. We are on a tight schedule."

Captain Blaine and her guards led Derren and Geller up to a set of double doors marked by a red 8. The doors parted, opening into a large oval room.

Derren was careful not to let his surprise show on his face. What were all these white-jacketed worker bees doing? But what caught his interest most was the pod, about the size of a human being, sitting atop an iron frame in the shape of a pyramid. Facing the pod, a few feet away, was a chair equipped with arm and leg restraints.

The chair's current occupant, a man with shiny brown hair corralled in a loose bun on top of his head, turned his watering wide eyes to Derren. He mumbled panicked words through his gag.

Derren looked to the figure behind the chair. Eleanor Latiff gave Derren a single glance with her piercing eyes and bent to check her captive's restraints.

"One of your psychics?" Derren asked. "I take it this one can't actually contact the dead either?"

He knew better than to say the name of Latiff's son, the one who'd died so young.

"Of course he can't." Latiff tugged extra hard on the strap across the man's chest. "But he'll be useful anyway."

Derren shrugged. Latiff's desperate attempts to contact her lost child were none of his affair. He was here to finish up the deal they'd begun so long ago. He scanned the room quizzically and then spoke. "I don't see my half of the trade?"

Anger shimmered across Latiff's face. "I will have it. Soon. It's not an easy task."

"Come, now. If I could create a demonic magician, gain control over an entire world, and get the Eye of Dedi," said Derren, "how hard can it be to fulfill your end of our deal?"

The door opened. A man in a white lab coat and slick black hair rushed into the room. He halted and stared at Derren.

"Derren," Latiff remarked coolly, "this is Dr. Coby."

Coby adjusted his round glasses. "Derren Fallow. In the flesh. I was beginning to think Latiff had invented you."

"Coby," Latiff said sharply. "Check the Proteus Pod."

She nodded at Derren. "A demonstration, perhaps, for the most skeptical magician I know."

Derren scrutinized the pod atop the iron pyramid. It had no visible seams. Only a small hollow on the front marred the smooth exterior. He knew exactly what that hollow was intended to hold.

"*This* is the device that will unlock the Eye?" Derren asked doubtfully.

Latiff nodded at the man tied to the chair. "With his help."

Derren lifted an eyebrow. "He actually has magical abilities?"

"Of course not. He's a fake like all the rest," Latiff answered. "But we've made a new discovery. It changes everything. Magic is nothing more than energy, energy that courses through all of us." Latiff eyed Derren as if watching for some reaction. "Some can naturally tap into that energy. We call them magicians," she went on. "But everyone has at least a little inside them. Most just don't know how to use it. That doesn't matter, however, because *I* do." Latiff returned to the pod and ran a finger along its back. The pod vibrated.

Derren took a step away from the humming contraption, watching as it was surrounded by a pulsing blue haze. The cloud twisted and spiraled around the iron pyramid before snaking toward the chair's struggling captive.

The blue energy enveloped the man, turning his skin translucent. His bones were visible, as if he'd become a living X-ray, and horror took over his face. As he writhed, tiny wormlike strands of light wriggled out of his body and swam back into the pod.

The man's struggles slowly ebbed. What was left of him sagged in the chair, looking like a dehydrated ghost. Derren had watched humans turned into the living skeletons called Rag-O-Rocs more times than he could count, but he had to admit that this startled even him.

"Is he—" he began to ask.

"Dead?" Latiff ran her hand over the man's shoulder. "No. Much worse."

Coby rushed past Derren to the pod, examining the small window designed to hold the Eye. "The subject is stuck between all planes of existence. The energy that once tethered him to our reality is gone. He barely exists, or perhaps doesn't exist at all. We're still researching that part."

Derren stared at the pod. "And with the energy you take from him . . . you're going to unlock the Eye?"

"From him and from people like him. You told me all about the Eye, Derren—how Dedi used it to create the entire Conjurian. A world for magicians. But he was just one man, however powerful he may have been. When I drain the life force from thousands, imagine what the Eye will do for me!"

Derren circled the floating globule of blue light that vaguely resembled the man who had been sitting in the chair. "And where are you going to get your thousands, my dear? Surely you can't get that many to sign up for your fake psychic contest."

Latiff smiled. "How many people do you think will flock here to witness the return of Angel Xavier?"

Derren shook his head. "I hate to be the bearer of bad news, but Angel Xavier has retired. Permanently."

Latiff kept smiling. "Fortunately no one will be at the show long enough to be disappointed."

CHAPTER 5

ALEX

Alex stood transfixed, staring at the monster who'd just burst into the clearing. Awen. This had to be Awen, the thing his parents had drawn in their journal. And they'd said it was immortal, which meant it couldn't die, which meant he was probably seeing exactly what his parents had seen. Was it some sort of tree zombie? Could trees even turn into zombies? It didn't seem likely, but . . .

The creature's two arms spanned fifteen feet long, and each ended in a wooden blade as long as one of Alex's forearms. The thing spun in place like an amusement ride designed by demons, and the arms swung toward them.

It was enough to wake Alex from his daze, and he leaped and rolled behind the ruins of a stone wall. Peeking out through a crack between two stones, he saw Pimawa bound right over Awen and land close to Savachia, who was still out cold. As if sensing the Jimjarian's intent to save the boy, Awen slammed an arm down between Pimawa and Savachia.

But while the monster was focused on Pimawa, Emma darted in, grabbing Savachia by the ankles and hauling him away. One of Awen's claws suddenly lashed out and sent Emma sprawling. Awen loomed over the girl, using her claw to pin Emma to the ground. A series of knocking noises burst from its mouth, as if it were full of woodpeckers trying to escape.

Okay. Alex was trying hard to trust that fate had led them into the path of this tree monster for a reason, but he wasn't about to let it squash his sister.

"Over here, tree-zilla," he yelled from behind his rock wall. The creature kept one wooden arm on Emma, but its head clicked around, watching as Alex jumped up and scuttled toward another tumbledown wall.

"Come on, you mutated oak!" Alex shook his arms. "I'm right here!"

Awen twisted its slender body to keep him in sight, its joints creaking. But it didn't release Emma. Pimawa hesitated, his eyes going from Alex to Emma to Awen.

Alex needed to capture more of the creature's attention. Digging in his pack until he found what he needed, he hopped out from behind his wall, hands held behind his back. He shuffled from side to side, edging closer to Awen.

"Let her go," said Alex. "Or we're going to play a little game called bonfire!" He brought his hands out from behind him, pointing the fireball shooter at Awen. He flexed his wrist. Sparks spewed from the device. With his other hand he stuffed wadded flash paper into the tube.

Awen hooked the wooden blade on the end of one of its arms through the collar of Emma's shirt. It backed away, dragging Emma toward the jungle.

Alex moved faster, closing the distance. He couldn't risk a fire while the beast still had his sister, but he couldn't let her take Emma into the jungle. All he had left to use was words, so he tried that.

"I don't want to do this," Alex told Awen, still holding the fireball shooter pointed right at the tree creature. "We didn't come here to hurt you. I have a feeling you don't want to hurt us. You would've done it by now." Alex searched the beast's face for understanding. "My parents thought you were important. Maybe you met them? Evelynne and Henry Mask—"

The creature jolted so suddenly, Alex tripped backward. His hand clenched around the weapon he held, and a fireball slammed into the ground between himself and Awen. Earthy-smelling smoke plumed up from the dry ground.

"Shoot!" Alex jumped as flames erupted by his feet. "No, no, no!"

Awen squealed like a cat through a megaphone. It dropped Emma and swatted with its enormous arms at the flames.

Alex moved back. "Emma! Get out of there!"

The beast continued sweeping the ground, hurling dirt and smoldering leaves in every direction. Freed, Emma scrambled to her feet and ran, dodging Awen's limbs and skipping around patches of flame.

Awen seemed to realize that putting out the fire was a lost cause. It rose to its full height, spread its arms, and roared, charging straight at Alex and Emma.

"Run, run!" shouted Alex.

"What do you think I'm doing?" Emma yelled.

They made it ten whole feet before Awen knocked them flat again. Wheezing, the siblings raised their arms to block the next attack.

To their surprise, Awen turned away from them. It planted both arms in the ground, and its upper body bent backward in a series of snapping jolts. And then, all movement stopped.

Alex and Emma watched in stunned silence as the monster froze. That's when they heard a click. The entire head of the creature swung open as if it were on hinges, and from

inside, a much smaller figure, shorter than Alex, leaped down to the ground. It was wrapped in a patchwork of cloth, its head a billowing mass of matted pale blond hair.

"Is that . . . ?" said Alex.

"A kid?" Emma finished. "Wait, it's a girl."

The girl had something in her hands like a flower vase. She ran toward the wall of flames and poured the water in the vessel over the fire.

"That's not going to work," Alex muttered. "There can't be more than two or three cups of water in there. . . ."

His voice trailed away as the girl kept pouring. An

impossible amount of water spilled from the container, and the crackling flames turned into hissing steam.

Once the fire was out, the girl continued pouring water, soaking the ground. Satisfied, she turned the vessel upright. Alex could tell from the way she cradled the cup that it was still full of water. She moved back to her wooden exoskeleton and, brushing locks of damp hair from her face, climbed inside.

"You're Awen?" asked Alex.

The girl didn't look at him. Instead, her gaze swept the jungle all around. Finally, she jabbed her finger at Alex, at herself, and at the jungle again. Stringy hair swinging, she nodded toward Savachia.

As though that settled it, she reached up and pulled the head of her tree-costume closed once again. The thing lumbered to life, striding across the clearing, scooping up Savachia without missing a step.

Securing his satchel on the run, Alex raced to catch up. "C'mon! She wants us to follow her."

"Wait, Alex!" said Emma. "We need to think this through."

"Emma, this is what we're *supposed* to do," said Alex impatiently. How could his sister still fail to get what was going on? "Besides, she's got Savachia."

Howls and cries came from the jungle behind them.

"Unless you want to wait here and find out what else is out there looking for a snack," Alex suggested to his sister. Then he sped off after Awen.

He glanced back to see Emma exchange an anxious glance

with Pimawa. But after another series of barks and grunts rose behind them, she nodded to Pim, and the two of them followed Alex and Awen.

In her tree suit, Awen seemed tireless. She headed uphill, and Alex, Emma, and Pimawa breathlessly tried to keep up. Aside from Savachia's occasional groaning, they trekked in silence.

Now and then, Awen halted and climbed from her cockpit to pluck flowers or spiky fruit from the overarching trees. Each time, she placed a finger to her lips, reminding her new companions to remain silent.

The odd companions climbed a small ridge and headed down into a valley. Through an occasional gap in the thick leaves, Alex could see a river far below. He had a guess where they were headed.

EMMA

Emma was panting for breath by the time they finally reached the water. Awen gently laid Savachia down on the bank before maneuvering her exoskeleton onto a raft of red bamboo anchored to a tree. The head of the tree-suit popped open, and Awen dropped from the body and began rummaging around various nooks of the raft.

Emma ran to Savachia's body. Pimawa's makeshift bandage had been soaked through, and the boy's shirt was wet with blood to the hem. His face was alarmingly pale.

"Do you have any medical supplies?" Emma asked. Pimawa peeled the sodden bandage away from Savachia's wound.

"Please," Emma implored Awen. "You must have something."

Awen carried on as though she hadn't heard. She continued searching the boat until, finally, she pulled out something that looked like a suitcase. Then she nodded and stepped back onto the grass, sidling between Emma and Pimawa to Savachia.

Awen's head cocked from side to side as she examined the wound. From a pouch around her waist, she removed the plants and fruits she had gathered on their journey, laying them out next to the boy. She opened the suitcase to reveal a variety of bowls, knives, and other tools.

Emma watched the girl's tiny hands deftly remove the spiky skin from the fruit. Awen smoothed the skin flat. Then she twisted three golden leaves together, tying them up with a slender sprout that was sturdier than it appeared.

As the girl worked, Emma felt guilt flush through her. Savachia looked inches away from death, and it was all her fault. She'd done it again. She'd tried to help, and all she'd managed to do was put her friends in danger. Emma watched the strange girl, placing what little hope she had into her hands.

The girl's hair whipped across her eyes, but Awen remained focused. She placed the skin of the fruit against Savachia's wound. With her free hand she grabbed an orange pod, squeezing its gooey contents around the fruit, gluing it in place.

Savachia's chest seemed to relax under Awen's touch. Awen nodded once more and turned her attention to mashing stringy blue plants in a mortar and pestle.

"Thank you," Emma said, never taking her eyes off Savachia. "Do you—do you talk?"

"Of course she talks," Alex snapped, poking his nose into Awen's bag. Her little brother had to be as tired as she was, Emma knew, but being exhausted did not make him less nosy. "Wow!" He held up a set of steel claws. "She probably hasn't had any contact with people in a long time," he went on in that irritating voice, as if he were a teacher giving a lecture. "That, combined with the full-time job of surviving"—Alex made a slashing motion with the claws—"probably makes talking an unnecessary luxury for her. Most of the time, anyway."

Awen didn't spare Alex a glance. Emma's heart skipped when the girl pivoted toward her. A smile shone from behind the matted hair as Awen held out three cups with a vibrant blue liquid inside.

Emma's throat was parched. But she hesitated. Awen did seem to be fairly kind. She was trying to take care of Savachia. But on the other hand, it wasn't that long ago that she'd had Emma pinned to the ground under her giant wooden claws. Should they really drink anything she was offering?

Alex didn't seem doubtful at all. He snatched a cup and chugged what was inside. Pimawa took his own cup with a polite bow. He sniffed at the liquid, took a sip, and then a longer drink.

Emma didn't understand how they could be so confident . . . until she took her own cup in her hand. It smelled better than any drink she'd ever had before. And she was so very thirsty. And what choice did they have, really, but to trust her?

Emma gulped down the drink, sweet but tangy, more refreshing than icy lemonade on a sweltering summer afternoon. Instantly she felt better than she had in days. Scratch that. Maybe ever.

She opened her mouth to thank Awen but found she couldn't speak. Emma watched in horror as the once-tiny girl in front of her began to stretch to five times her height. Panicked, Emma scrambled to her feet, only to fall face-first onto the soft grass. She turned her head, glimpsing her brother and Pimawa sprawled unconscious next to her, and then the darkness took her.

CHAPTER 6

EMMA

Emma's stomach sloshed side to side with a sickening motion. Her eyes cracked open. The world matched her stomach's rhythm, bobbing up and down. Despite the ache in her limbs, Emma forced her eyes all the way open. Her head lay against something hard. Bars! She was in a cage on the raft!

On the other side of the bars, the jungle slipped past. The raft was moving steadily downstream. Taking a deep breath, Emma tried to pull herself up. But she fell back. Her legs were still asleep.

Awen was seated at the prow of the boat, in her wooden armor once more. The head was open, and Emma could see the girl's thin frame inside the cockpit as she worked the suit's levers. Its branching arms swept into and then out of the frothing river like paddles, propelling them forward.

To where? Emma rolled onto her stomach and pulled herself forward. Alex was out next to her. Pimawa lay on his side, ears flopping between bars.

"Where's Savachia?" asked Emma.

"Your—companion—is—safe," said Awen. Each word came out slowly and stiffly, as if she had not used her mouth for talking in many, many years.

"*Now* she speaks," Emma muttered. Then she retched.

"Lie still," said Awen, her words coming a little more smoothly than before. "The effects will wear off soon."

"You drugged us," said Emma, wiping stringy spit from the corner of her mouth. "Why?"

"You are bait," said Awen simply.

That didn't help the queasy sensation in Emma's belly. "I'm sorry, bait for what?"

"Henry. Evelynne," said Awen. "They will return for you. I make them come back." Despite the girl's mechanical speech pattern, the touch of anger was crystal clear.

"I don't understand," said Emma. "Why do you want our parents to come back here?"

Awen turned her face, a flash of rage in her brown eyes. "They promised to cure me."

"Cure you of what?" asked Emma.

Awen slammed the levers harder, driving the raft faster through the rugged currents.

"That's it?" said Emma. "Two sentences, and you forget how to talk again?"

Awen didn't say another word. Irritated, Emma crawled over to Pimawa, tugging his ears out from between the bars. Turning to check on her brother, she found him sitting up, holding his belly.

"You okay?" asked Emma.

"Aside from my stomach trying to strangle my kidneys," muttered Alex, "I'm great."

"I don't know where she's taking us," said Emma. "We have to get out of here."

Alex squinted at the shimmering water. "And what, drown?" He rested his back against the bars. "She's had an experience with the Eye." He said it loudly, making sure Awen could hear him. She did.

Awen's feral gaze snapped around, burrowing into Alex. She jerked the levers, causing the suit's arms to smash the water harder.

Alex gave her a smile that looked sincere. "I've had one too," he told her, as casually as if he were on a cruise admiring the scenery.

"What're you talking about, Alex?" asked Emma.

But Alex ignored her, the way he always did when he was trying to figure something out.

"I read about you—in my parents' journals," he said to Awen. "You should have gone with them, I think."

"Safer here," said Awen. She paddled even faster. The raft launched forward, narrowly missing an outcropping of rock.

"Where did our parents go?" asked Alex.

The raft moved at a frightening speed. The jungle ahead parted, revealing open sea.

"Alex," whispered Emma. "Are you—is she—were our parents really here?"

"Of course they were," Alex answered impatiently. "I keep *telling* you. They were on this island. They drew a picture of Awen in their journal. The question is, where did they go when they left here? Awen?"

"You should know," Awen snapped. She yanked one lever forward, the other back. The raft spun sideways, shooting around the mouth of the river, careening toward the rocky shoreline. Emma yelped. At the last moment, Awen swung the raft around a tongue of rock, and they slipped into a placid cove.

A wall of smooth rock surrounded the inlet. A black opening, half submerged, loomed like an empty eye socket.

"What's in there?" asked Emma, eyeing the darkness nervously.

"Your parents," said Awen.

"They're *here*? In that cave?" A jolt of shock and longing and something almost like terror shot Emma to her feet.

"I have you," said Awen. "They will come. I have time." She smiled menacingly.

"I bet there's a gateway in there!" Alex pressed his face against the bars. "Like the passageway at Tower of Dedi! That's how Mom and Dad traveled here!"

Emma winced at the memory of the now-destroyed Tower.

"But who puts a gateway in the middle of nowhere?" Alex carried on. "And how will our parents know you have us?"

A loud crackle interrupted his questions, and a burst of blue light erupted from the cave. Emma dropped to the floor. The light faded. Inside the cave, something splashed. A voice shouted urgent words Emma could not quite understand.

"I guess they know," muttered Alex.

"Are you serious?" Emma yanked on the bars. How could Alex be so calm? "Mom! Dad!" Emma called to her parents in desperation.

To her shock, Emma spotted movement up ahead. She opened her mouth to yell again but stopped herself. If her parents did come out of that cave, would Awen kill them all? Should Emma call to her parents to hurry, or warn them to run?

Awen tensed. She sniffed the air. Dark figures stumbled out of the mouth of the cave, clinging to rocks or staggering as a rush of water came with them.

Those were not Emma's parents. They were men dressed in black body armor. Soldiers? Guards? Disappointment and confusion swirled in Emma's brain as Awen turned toward her prisoners.

"You!" the blond girl snarled. "You brought them here!"

"What?" sputtered Emma, bewildered. "We don't even know who those people are!"

With a low growl, Awen reached down, hauling the top half of the suit over her. The wooden armor creaked, rising on bent knees. It emitted a haunting battle cry before plunging into the river, wooden arms dragging it through the water to the cave.

"What is she doing?" asked Emma. "Who are those men?"

"I don't . . ." Alex trailed off as though unable to believe what he was seeing.

"Are they Tower guards?" Emma pressed. "Maybe Derren sent them from Conjurian City to look for us."

Alex shook his head. "Unless he had time to upgrade their uniforms, I don't think they're from Conjurian City."

Awen had nearly reached the men, still struggling in the water. "Should we warn them?" asked Emma.

"Are we on *their* side?" said Alex.

"I have no clue. And since we don't know—" Emma grabbed the lock of the cage. "Get us out of here. We'll get Savachia, then go back to the carriage. Alex!" Her brother couldn't help staring at the sight of Awen tearing through the water toward the soldiers. Emma rattled the lock again. "Alex, open it!"

ALEX

"Okay, okay!" Alex grabbed the lock and saw it was crudely forged from metal. "Haven't seen one like this before, but it's pretty basic. Shouldn't be hard." He pulled his sock down. A small pouch with his lock-picking tools was strapped to his ankle.

"Where'd you get that?" asked Emma.

"It was a going-away present from Christopher Agglar," said Alex, grinning at the thought of the old magician. He had his faults, but old Agglar had still taught Alex a thing or two.

Alex ignored the distant yells and the sound of lumber slamming on rock. Awen must have reached the shore. He twisted the picks. The iron of the lock was aged with flaking rust.

"Alex! Hurry!" said Emma.

"Yeah, thanks. I'm not exactly taking a lunch break." Alex slid in two more picks. Based on the age of the lock, he guessed that he'd need more leverage to—

Ker-chunk!

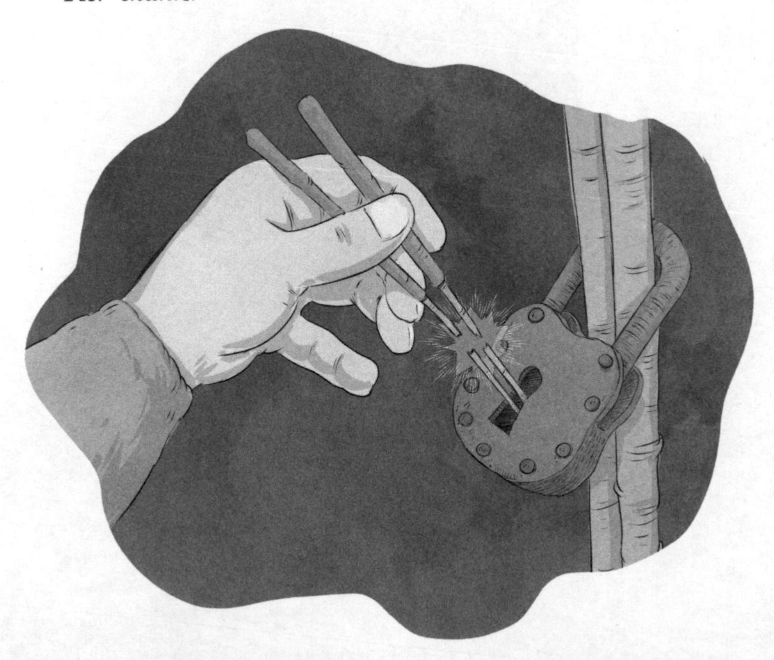

“Dang!” Alex withdrew his mangled picks.

“Alex!” hissed Emma.

“Not now, Emma!” Alex pulled out his final pick and slid it into the lock. Last chance. He didn’t dare say that aloud.

Emma had turned to Pimawa, shaking him. She gasped and then grabbed Alex’s shoulder.

The pick slipped out of the lock. “Emma! What’re you—”

Then Alex looked where Emma was pointing. A kite-shaped monstrosity had broken through the water’s surface, and now it slammed into the cage. A belly full of teeth gnashed at the bars. Before Alex could even yell with surprise, the raft capsized, plunging the cage into the cold, murky water below.

CHAPTER 7

DERREN

Derren followed Latiff out of the lab and into a darkened room nearby. The only light came from the illuminated glass displays. He paused at a glass tube. Inside, a dummy hung upside down, strapped into a straitjacket.

"That was Houdini's," said Latiff casually, as if it were of no more importance than an old sweater. She walked on into the shadows.

Derren took his time catching up, taking in the priceless artifacts Latiff had collected in her private museum. Wands, a zigzag woman illusion, Thurston's floating head table.

"I must thank you," said Latiff, stopping next to a case of scrolls, stone tablets, and flaking old books. "Without the knowledge you provided to Sanctum, we would never have made it to this moment."

"My pleasure." Derren scanned the room for an exit. "We're on the same team, after all."

"Are we?" Latiff strolled along the wall of artifacts, her footsteps echoing.

Derren shrugged. "I was hoping we could conclude our deal," he told Latiff. "How soon do you expect to have my half of the trade?"

Before Derren could answer, a door clicked open, blinding Derren with a shaft of white light. Captain Blaine darted to Latiff, whispering something in her ear.

"Wait no longer." Latiff beamed at Derren. "I have your half of the bargain."

Two more guards entered, wheeling a squeaky hospital gurney. Strapped on top was a young girl, her dirty hair cascading over the side. Her clothes were tattered, her face masked in dirt and clotted blood, her eyes closed.

"As promised." Latiff waved dismissively at the child. "And now you have your half of the bargain with you?"

"As promised?" Derren inspected the girl. "Locked up like a wild animal is not what we agreed. Is she even alive?"

"Do you even have the Eye?" Latiff planted her feet.

Derren stepped toward her, pulling his sleeves up, showing both sides of his hands. He grasped her hand, turning it palm up, and waved his hand over hers, once, twice. On the third pass a tiny pebble appeared resting on her palm. And there it was: the Eye of Dedi.

Latiff closed her hand around the Eye.

"Abracadabra," Derren scoffed. Walking lightly as if embarking on a Sunday stroll, he headed for the exit, calling back, "Bring the girl. I'll take care of the transportation. Obviously you had a hard enough time finding her."

"About that." Latiff's voice hit Derren like an icicle in his back. “Did it slip your mind to mention that the Maskelyne children were with Awen on that island?”

Derren casually stopped. “My dear, as has happened many times in our past, I have not the faintest inkling of what you’re talking about.”

Latiff smiled. “Truly? I’m shocked. You were, of course aware, that the Maskelyne boy activated the Eye? That would seem to be information you would want to pass along. You have provided us with so much knowledge. Unfortunately, it seems, you held back the best for yourself. If the boy can unlock the Eye, why not bring him to me? Unless of course, you know more than you are sharing?”

Derren didn’t have a chance to move before the guards closed in on him. Latiff turned into the shadows. “Captain Blaine, cancel Mr. Fallow’s suite reservation. He’ll be staying down here, where we can put him in a more sharing mood.”

CHAPTER 8

ALEX

Air bubbles blinded Alex. The world spun upside down, cold and wet. He kept both hands on the lock, the only chance of escape. If his last pick slipped out, it was over. He fought the panic, the urge to breathe, knowing he wasn't destined to die here. Fate wasn't finished with him yet.

Twisting the lock one way and the pick the other, Alex finally felt something give. He yanked hard and the lock fell away. Lungs searing, Alex shoved the gate open.

Freedom was so close, but Alex groped blindly back into the cage until his fingers caught something soft: Emma's sweatshirt. He pulled on it with all his strength and dragged Emma out into the river. She just managed to slip her hands

under Pimawa's arms. Great! That was all three of them. He let go of Emma, and she thrashed her way toward where the water shimmered with light.

Alex was ready to follow his sister to the surface and air—sweet, marvelous air! But suddenly the light vanished, as if a dirty white sheet had been thrown over his head.

A sheet with gnashing teeth in the middle of it.

Alex kicked as hard as he could, but the sea creature wrapped its fins around him. His arms felt weak; his legs were limp. He had been too long without air. Too long . . .

As the creature hugged him tighter, Alex's arms were

crushed to his sides. He felt his hand press against the pocket of his cargo shorts. Of course! He wasn't destined to die here—he'd always known.

Alex wormed his fingers into his pocket and hoped that woofle seeds worked in water.

The creature's teeth clamped down, just missing Alex's head as he grasped a handful of the seeds. Alex let them loose into the water, and they floated like enticing food. The creature snatched at the seeds with that hungry mouth, and its grip loosened.

Seizing the opportunity, Alex kicked free and went tumbling into the current . . . and right into something soft and smooth. Alex grabbed on to whatever he could hold. He didn't know or care what he was clinging to because it was pulling him up to the light and the air, and that was all that mattered.

His head broke the surface, and that first gulp of air was the greatest sensation he had ever felt. The next sensation was the worst: Alex was still traveling higher.

He was holding on to the back fin of a giant fish. But this fish didn't seem to think that staying in the water was a good idea. What kind of a fish could actually fly?

This kind, apparently. The fish soared above the river, angling toward land. If Alex was going to let go, he had to time it perfectly, hoping he would land where it was too shallow to get eaten again but deep enough to prevent snapping his legs—or his neck!

But before Alex could calculate the optimal time to jump, the fish puffed out like a kite full of air and bucked him off toward the rock face.

"Ahh!" Alex yelled, sailing through the air. "I was getting off anyway!"

Alex splashed into a shallow tidal pool, only remaining in it long enough to catch his breath before he scrambled for dry land. A few yards away, Emma hauled Pimawa up onto the shore. Alex crawled over and collapsed next to them as the water behind them suddenly exploded in a plume of froth and seaweed.

"What was that?" gasped Emma.

"Conclusive proof that woofle seeds can ignite underwater," Alex wheezed. "How is Pimawa?"

Pimawa shot upright with a watery cough.

"I think whatever Awen drugged us with affects Jimjarians

more than humans," said Emma, patting Pimawa's back. "Are you okay?"

"Enough," Alex replied. "Have you seen Awen?"

"No," said Emma. "And those men are gone too. Who were they, and how did they get here? And *where* did they go?"

"No idea." Alex looked around, trying to orient himself. They were huddled on a thin scrap of beach, the only sandy part of the entire cove. The cave that the black-clad soldiers had come out had to be around the rocky point to his right. He left his sister and Pim sitting where they were and ventured over to peer around the point.

Yes, the cave was there and it was empty. Pieces of Awen's tree suit bobbed in the water. Alex reached out and snagged a belt pouch as it drifted past. Empty. The only clue was a metal emblem sewn into the fabric.

Alex brought his find back to the other two. "Ever hear of *SANCTUM*?" he asked, dropping the pouch on the sand.

"Can't say that I have." Pimawa got to his feet with Emma's help.

"We have to find out what's in that cave," Alex asserted. "It'll be our next clue. I'm sure of it."

Emma rolled her eyes, but at least she didn't argue. The three of them edged around the point and waded into the cave's mouth. A strong current swirled past their knees. Alex peered inside.

"It's really dark," he said, waiting for his eyes to adjust. The water echoed. The world slowly began to take shape until, "There!" On a shelf of rock about a foot above the water was a shallow rectangular box about the size of a doorway.

"It's the gateway!" Alex breathed.

"Are you sure?" asked Emma, peering in beside him.

"Of course," said Alex. "That must be how those Sanctum soldiers got here. It's also how they left—and how they took Awen."

"Probably for the best," said Pimawa, removing his coat and wringing it out. "Dedi knows what else she had in store for us."

"We'll ask once we find her." Alex dragged up a Sanctum backpack bobbing in the water. "Let's look in here. See if there's anything we might need."

"Alex!" Emma ripped the bag out of his hands. "We have to help Savachia!"

Alex pondered the idea for a moment. "Yeah, you're right, Em. No problem. You two head back. I'll go after Awen."

"Stop it!" Emma grabbed his sweatshirt. "You have no idea—"

"What I'm doing?" said Alex. "C'mon, Em! You heard her! *She knows where our parents went!*"

"If you—"

Blue light crackled from the cave. All three of them jumped as the familiar blue light reflected off the water.

"The gateway's opening!" cried Alex.

"Those men are coming back for us," gasped Emma.

"Hide quickly!" Pimawa helped Emma wade toward the beach.

But Alex moved farther into the cave. It made little sense that the men would reappear. They'd gotten what they wanted—Awen. It had to be someone else coming through the gateway this time.

Then he heard splashing. A familiar voice cried:

"Buttersnaps! Maybe you could have mentioned the water. I would have worn galoshes."

Alex grinned at Emma and Pimawa. He could see that they recognized the speaker too.

"Hordes of hogshead!" echoed the voice. "These pantaloons are brand-new and, I might add, not waterproof, Clive!"

Alex leaned into the cave. "Hey! Are you guys lost?"

Clive Grubian, the most beautiful ruffian and undercover agent Alex had ever known, strode out of the shadows with his brother, Neil, sitting on his shoulders.

"One might ask you the same question, young Maskelyne," said Neil with a chuckle.

Clive's long legs made easy work of stepping through the water, getting himself and Neil onto dry land. The other three followed.

Neil grinned fiendishly at Emma and Pimawa. "What are the odds? All of us lost and then found in the same spot?"

"The odds were actually one hundred percent," said Alex. "All five of us are *supposed* to be here. Nowhere else we could be."

"Hooligan's hollow earth, the boy has blossomed with confidence," said Neil.

"Try not to mention it," muttered Emma.

Neil embraced Emma and Pimawa with squishy hugs. "And before we continue this fortuitous reunion, may I ask the whereabouts of my Gertie?"

"She's fine," said Pimawa, picking a clump of seaweed off his jacket.

"A few minor dings," said Alex. "Nothing I can't fix."

"And our beloved street urchin?" asked Neil.

"We need to get back to him," said Emma. "He's . . . not well."

"Then we best get a-movin'," said Neil. He eyed the slender wooden blade his brother had just picked up from the sand. "I'd say there're a few details you must explain along the way."

EMMA

Emma, Alex, and Pimawa led the Grubians out of the cove and over the rocky crags. They wound their way inland along the riverbank. The overhanging foliage trapped the humidity, and it hung over the group like a warm, moist towel swarming with bugs.

Emma walked close to the water's edge, keeping a wary eye on the jungle. Who knew what else might leap out of there? Pimawa seemed to be worried too. He kept close by her side.

Alex, though? Alex ran ahead, chasing six-legged lizards. "We're going to find Savachia, Em, no worries!" he called to his sister.

"Come farther up the bank, young lady," said Neil after Emma slipped for the sixth time. "We are fresh out of life preservers."

Emma shook her head. "Imps. They might come back."

"Emma is correct," said Pimawa, helping steady her. His eyes remained fixed on the jungle.

"Ha! Ta, ha!" Neil wagged his finger at his brother, who was walking stooped over to avoid the drooping vines.

Clive removed two glass jars from his jacket pocket, handing them to his brother.

"Strawberry jelly," said Neil, shaking a jar in each hand. "You can tame imps with the stuff." He passed them back to his brother. Emma was much too groggy to ask exactly how he knew that, and Pimawa didn't seem to care.

Neil obliged them anyway. "In our past career, we once stole—er—acquired a truckload of jelly. In our haste to get away—ah—I mean make our delivery, someone improperly set our gateway destination." Neil shot an annoyed look at Clive. Clive shrugged. "The truck dropped into a marsh, smack-dab in the middle of a tribe of starving imps. As we had no other weapons, we hurled several dozen jars at our attackers. They grew quite surprisingly cooperative after that. We bribed them with the rest of the jelly into pulling our truck free. Quite handy, really. We haven't traveled without it since."

"Tell us about the Conjurian City," said Alex, who seemed to have grown bored with the elusive lizards. "How's the rebuilding going?"

"I daresay," said Neil, taking a breather against a dead tree, "Master Derren has done more for the city in the past month than the Circle had in centuries."

"How did he get it all done?" asked Emma.

"Mostly by doing nothing," said Neil with a chuckle, wiping his forehead with a threadbare handkerchief. "Aside from arbitrating the occasional squabble here and there, he's let the people get about the business of being people. His belief in them alone has done wonders for morale."

Feeling a little safer now that she knew about the jelly trick, Emma moved onto less squishy ground. "And he put you two in charge of M.A.G.E.?"

"Specifically, in charge of locating all the illegal gateways into the Conjurian for the Magic Antiquities Guardianship Enforcement," Neil confirmed. "We are registering the portals, including the one that led us to you. And lucky it did. Seems like you lot were in a spot of trouble back there."

"A bit," Pimawa admitted.

"Look!" Alex shouted from ahead. Emma's heart jumped into her throat but then settled back into its rightful place when she saw that her brother wasn't being eaten or captured, but rather pointing at a large skull.

It was a carving of a skull upon closer inspection, created from a single massive tree trunk. It had been balanced over the water on a pylon of spears, the sharp ends protruding up to support the massive form.

"That carving looks like the same wood that made Awen's exoskeleton. I bet we're close to wherever she lives," Alex said.

"My, what a charming welcome mat," murmured Neil.

"Do you think Savachia could be there?" Emma asked.

"There's no telling what Awen got up to while we were unconscious," Pimawa admitted. "It's certainly worth checking out."

Emma could see a faint path worn along the riverbank. Alex charged ahead, shouting at the rest of them to hurry up.

They followed.

CHAPTER 9

EMMA

It took a bit of finagling—and Emma falling in the lake, twice—but Alex rigged up a makeshift raft from deadwood that was just seaworthy enough to get the group to the skull. Five thin stone pillars speckled with purple and red jutted up around the massive tree. Its substantial trunk was the color of sandstone and made Emma think of another enormous tree.

"Reminds me of Plomboria," said Pimawa.

Emma smiled back at him, pretending she was thinking the same thing.

Floating at the base, they decided Clive should be the first to climb the ladder into Awen's dwelling, seeing as how he was the biggest and, by Pimawa's account, the most intimidating. And although she didn't say it, Emma couldn't bear to be the first to find Savachia—if he was there at all. There was no telling what his condition might be.

Clive went in without hesitation. They waited for him to signal with three loud stomps if the coast was clear.

"What's the signal if it's not clear?" asked Emma.

"The sound of Clive thrashing on the floor as whatever monster's in there tears him apart." Neil had a wide grin, as if proud of his little joke. Emma didn't laugh.

But the next thing they heard wasn't a stomp or a scream. Instead, it was a voice. "Hey! Where'd you guys go? Get up here!"

Emma felt herself go almost boneless with relief. Savachia!

"Well, gracious," said Neil. "That young man takes mortal wounds in stride."

They all rushed for the ladder, arriving on the first landing in time to see Clive stomping on the floor. With a baffled look on his face, he watched all three of them push past him to the second level.

They climbed a narrow staircase made from sanded branches, barely wide enough for Pimawa. Emma reached the second floor first and stopped so suddenly her brother's face slammed into her backside.

"Ow," said Alex. "Emma, keep moving." But as he came up the ladder, he became as awed as she was.

The room had four sides but no right angles. Almost every inch was filled with carved figures, ranging from crude dolls made out of shells and bamboo to four-foot statues of what appeared to be hooded monks. The older carvings, sitting along the walls, had been overcome by moss and brown

mold, while the latest ones had elaborate details and were arranged in a cramped circle, as if in the midst of an ancient ceremony. A squat table sat by the window.

Savachia was crouched by the circle of statues, studying them intently. "Please tell me those don't live on the island," he said.

Emma stared at him. He looked . . . fine. She could still see the rip in his bloody shirt, but the way he was moving? And acting? You'd never know he'd been hurt. She was almost annoyed. She'd been so worried for nothing.

"It's possible," said Alex, gently tapping a statue's teeth. "Some sort of lion hybrid? Pim, have you seen a creature like th—"

Pimawa gazed at the statue, frozen, ears drooped behind his head.

"Pim?" asked Emma.

"Wograth," squeaked Pimawa.

"Wog what?" asked Savachia.

Shaking off his surprise, Pimawa edged away from the statue. "They're not real. Wograths, they are, well, a Jimjarian version of the boogeyman. They're . . . guardians."

"Guardians of what?" Emma asked with interest.

"Hmmm . . . to be honest, I don't exactly know," Pimawa admitted. "We only whispered about them when I was a kid. If you stepped out of line, the Wograths would get you. That's what we told each other."

"How would Awen know about them?" asked Emma.

"Who knows? I'm just glad you're going to get me out of here." Savachia stepped to the edge of the circle, but as

he went to cross the ring, his heel nicked one of the statues, causing a domino effect. Statues tumbled everywhere, but miraculously only one shattered, spraying clay fragments at their feet.

Alex slipped past his sister before Savachia could say anything. A thick book lay open in the dust. Alex picked it up cautiously.

"What is that?" asked Savachia.

Alex cradled the book in his hands. It had a rough bark cover, bound by thin, twisted vines. Holding it together the best he could, he set it on the small table in the corner. Emma watched as he turned each fragile page with surgical care. The ink was a deep, aged brown, forming shaky symbols.

Alex traced the spiral of symbols across the paper. "These symbols. It's the same language in the tunnels under the Tree of Dedi. They match the ones Mom and Dad copied into their journal."

Savachia peered over Alex's shoulder to get a closer look. Emma hung back.

Alex leaned closer to the book. "I knew it. I knew it! It's our next clue! This is why Mom and Dad came to the island. *This* is the reason why fate brought us here!"

"Makes sense." Savachia shrugged at Emma. "Fate dragged us through sea monsters and hurricanes and imps to find a dusty book in a weird girl's house filled with a language no one can read. Quite the joker, that fate."

Alex ignored him, flipping back and forth through the pages. Growing impatient, Emma leaned over his shoulder. "Will it help us find Mom and Dad?" she demanded. Alex was obsessed with fate right now, she knew that. But she didn't have to agree with him to find this book . . . interesting.

"I don't know. I mean yes, it will. Eventually. If we can decipher it." Alex closed the book gently. "Or find someone who can decipher it. I told you, Em. We have to go after Awen."

Alex rose and tucked the book under his arm. "It's her book. Presumably she can read it. She has to be why we were brought here. We need to find her."

"Stop it, Alex," Emma said shortly. "We're in way over our heads. We don't even know who took her or where they went. Besides, we're supposed to be looking for Mom and Dad. Or have you lost interest in that petty quest?"

Closing his eyes, Alex shook his head. "Of course I want to find Mom and Dad, but we need Awen to translate this book so we *can* find them!"

"You're jumping to conclusions so fast you might as well be a kangaroo!" Emma snapped. "The old Alex would've figured out what that book says before blindly running off after some wild kid who almost killed us."

"And the old Emma would have run off on a quest faster than I could say magic!" Alex snapped back.

Emma's lips tightened. Her voice dropped. "Well, I know better now. For once you should listen to me. I *do* know a little something about charging headlong into danger with only hope as a weapon—and the consequences when it doesn't work out."

"Emma," said Pimawa, "are you okay?"

"No," said Emma. "We shipwrecked, I almost killed Savachia, and a pack of invisible gremlins almost ate us."

"Imps, technically," said Neil. He had walked close to Alex, peering over his shoulder. "They get mean if you call them gremlins."

"This is impossible. We're running around, risking our lives chasing folktales!" Emma's voice echoed in the cramped space.

Neil picked up a clay head and gave it a smooch. "What do you say we all go downstairs and scrounge ourselves up a little repast? Maybe some twigs with a side of caterpillars."

Emma fumed. "Savachia needs to get checked out by a real doctor. We should go back to Conjurian City and come up with a plan. Find someone who can read that book. Someone who's *not* Awen," Emma added before Alex could retort.

"I'm fine!" Savachia slapped his side, looking down at the dark stain on his shirt. "I could use a new outfit is all."

"See?" said Alex. "He's all right. And we don't have time to waste, going all the way back to Conjurian City. Emma, we were supposed to find this book. We have to keep going." Alex held the book out as if to solidify his case. A loose parchment slipped out from between the pages and drifted to the floor.

"What is that?" asked Neil.

Alex snatched it up. It was much newer than the book,

and had been made from pressed leaves, a patchwork of faded green. The message, however, was clear and stunning. "Whoa!"

"What?" Emma nudged past Savachia. "What does it say?"

"Look for yourself." Alex held the scrap up to Emma.

"I told you Mom and Dad knew Awen."

Emma stared openmouthed at the journal. Her parents' names were clearly there . . . but something wasn't right about what Alex was saying.

"Alex, that book is ancient. Awen's just a kid. She couldn't have written that."

Alex shook his head. "Of course she could. She's immortal."

Emma gaped at him. "What did you say?"

"Awen's immortal. Mom and Dad wrote it in their journal," Alex said cheerfully. "She's probably been living here for who knows how long? Centuries. She carved all this, I bet!" He waved a hand at the statues and dolls.

Emma couldn't take much more of this nonsense. Alex actually seemed to believe what he was saying.

Savachia shook his head. "But what does *find Blackstone* mean?" Emma twitched in surprise as he came to lean over her shoulder. "Are you saying Awen thinks your parents went to find Harry Blackstone? But he's been dead for ages."

"Not the magician," said Pimawa, finally building up the nerve to move past the statues. "Blackstone is a place."

"Where?" asked Emma. "If that's where Mom and Dad went, then that's where we're going. Not"—she gave her little brother a stern look—"after Awen."

"Blackstone is a legend." Pimawa curled his lip.

"How come we've never heard of it before?" said Neil, popping up from behind the statues.

"Simple," said Pimawa. "It's a Jimjarian legend. It's where the Wograths live. And like them, it's not real."

Emma threw up her hands, nearly smacking Savachia in the face. "So there's your prize, Alex. Fate brought you all the way here so a wild jungle girl that you think can live *forever* could reveal that Mom and Dad went to an imaginary place populated by Jimjarian ghost stories. Maybe we should head to Never Neverland next. Or look for Mom and Dad in the Land of Oz."

Alex and Emma glowered at one another with the ferocity that only siblings can muster. Then two large hands holding jelly jars rose from the stairwell opening.

"Just in time, Clive!" Neil clapped. "Soooo we've decided? Patch up our poor little Gertie and head back to Conjurian City. I'm sure Clive and I, given our new positions, could wrangle up a new ship, fully crewed. Seeking artifacts is in our new job description, you know. All expenses would be covered, of course."

"The sooner, the better," said Emma, pushing Clive's jar-laden hands out of her way and storming downstairs.

"Good talk," said Neil. "At least we're not all stuck on an island together." Once again, he was the only one laughing.

"She'll come around." Alex balanced Awen's book on his head as he went down the stairs too.

"To what?" Savachia followed him.

Emma spent the rest of the afternoon sitting on the dock. Neil and Clive scavenged a decent-sized meal from the stores of dried meats and vegetables, but Emma ignored them when they called her to eat. She was hungry, but she was also angry and confused and couldn't tolerate listening to her brother jabber on and on about fate guiding them.

After all they had survived, they still had nothing to show for it. A note scrawled by an unpredictable jungle girl about their parents going to an imaginary place? She had read more believable plots in children's books. She sighed, and since she couldn't figure out what to think, she settled on not thinking at all. Instead, she watched a two-headed dragonfly hover over a patch of orange flowers.

Footsteps behind her wobbled the dock. She turned to see Savachia had found a new shirt, sewn from homemade silk. She turned back, searching for the dragonfly.

"You should eat." Savachia held out a hunk of something dried wrapped in a leaf. "I think it's jerky. Or tree bark. Not sure." She didn't react. He placed the snack down beside her. "You know, everything I've done since I can remember was to help my mom. This is the closest thing to a vacation I've had in my life."

"How is she?" asked Emma, feeling guilty. She'd known all about his mother being sick—very sick—back in the place that magicians called the Flatworld and that she had always called home.

He smiled, then spat a wad of leaf into the water. A fish ballooned up to the surface, enveloping the chunk, dragging it down into the murky water. "The same. The doctors say it's only a matter of time."

"I'm sorry," said Emma.

"Don't be," Savachia answered. "They've been saying that for years now."

"I know you came with us because you hoped the Eye could cure her, if we could just figure out how it worked," Emma admitted. "We failed."

"Nah." Savachia leaned over, swishing his hand in the lake. Several more of the parachute-like fish drifted up. "You remember all that stuff that happened back in the city? Sorry. Yeah. You're not likely to forget. I meant, when I helped Alex take out that Conjurer guy, I realized it was the first time I'd helped someone other than my mom or myself." He lay back on the dock, clasping his hands under his head. "Thanks to you. And I guess thanks to your little preacher brother with all his destiny mumbo jumbo. That doesn't guarantee I'll find a cure for my mom. But it has given me hope."

Despite her best efforts not to, Emma smiled at Savachia. His gaze, however, was distant.

Emma picked up the leaf with the meat rolled inside it. She took a bite. It wasn't half-bad. A few more chews and she felt a little better. Then she saw Savachia smiling at her too.

"Look," said Savachia. "I know your brother used to be a book nerd, and now he's a woo-woo serendipity nerd, but I'm starting to believe him."

Emma retracted her smile. "Seriously?" But after all, Savachia was trying to save his mom. Maybe he'd believe in anything that could give him a hint of hope.

"I know what you're thinking," said Savachia. "I'm not being naive. But consider everything that's happened. We found this island. I get stabbed but get rescued by Tarzan's daughter who just happens to be able to heal my wound. We find a mystery book with a note telling us your parents were definitely here." Savachia leaned back on his elbows. "All of that has to add up to something. I don't know if Awen's been alive for centuries or not. I don't know if Blackstone is real or not. I don't know if your parents actually went there or not. But I do know that girl knows *something*. She knows enough for those goons to kidnap her."

Emma gave him a quick, wry look. "We don't know anything about those people that took her," said Emma. "Other than they were much better equipped than us."

"We know they want whatever it is she knows," said Savachia. "And I'm betting it is the same thing your parents were after."

Emma sighed. "You really think Alex is right? We should try to find Awen?"

Savachia nodded.

It was a foolish idea. The faintest of faint hopes. Emma had tried taking a leap of faith before, and it'd had disastrous results. Could she really bear to risk it all again?

Emma watched the dragonflies, fearless in their flights. At last she brushed her hands off and stood.

"We'll need weapons." Emma held out her hand to Savachia. "You coming?" Savachia grabbed hold, and the two raced back to the hut.

CHAPTER 10

ALEX

Holding her supply sack over her head, Emma followed Alex into the cave. Pimawa and Savachia came next, with the Grubians taking up the rear. The low tide smacked at the rocks sheltering the inlet.

"The tide is coming in," said Alex. "We won't have much time."

They slogged their way toward the gateway, every sound echoing off the slimy rock walls. Neil, perched on his brother's shoulders, leaned over and inspected the tall, narrow box balanced on the rock ledge. It was about the size of a doorway, with a panel on the front that seemed meant to swing outward.

"Seen this kind before," said Neil. "A smugglers' gate." Neil slapped the top of the box, then ran his fingers around the edges.

"A what?" Emma rubbed her arms nervously. Neil continued stroking the contraption while he explained.

"Smugglers' gates drop you in a random location every time you pass through. Makes it a lot easier to shake a tail. This one"—Neil pressed his ear to the doorway—"thankfully only has a few destinations locked in. Better odds of ending up wherever they took the girl." Neil patted the top of his brother's head. Clive put him down. Yanking up his pantaloons, Neil tiptoed along the rock pedestal holding the gateway.

"Just enough juice for one more trip, it seems," said Neil. "You'll have to be quick in case it dies."

Savachia jerked to a halt. "What if those Sanctum people destroyed the gateway on the other side?"

"Oh," said Neil, as if the thought had just occurred to him. "Then you die."

"What?" shouted Pimawa.

"Simple gateway physics, really," said Neil. "Every gateway must have a destination gateway. Otherwise you end up drifting around in the ether until you dissolve." Neil noticed the concerned looks on his audience's faces. "Or so I'm told. Not to worry! As I said. If this is a smugglers' gateway, it has multiple destinations. Those goons wouldn't be able to destroy all of them. One way or another, you'll end up someplace."

"Great pep talk," groused Savachia.

"We'll be fine," said Alex, forging ahead in the water. "We'll get to where we're supposed to be."

Now it was Emma's turn to groan.

The water splashed higher around Neil's legs. "Best get a move on before we all drown." He opened the front panel. Blue light drifted out, reflecting off the water and rock walls.

Pimawa insisted on going first, just in case those men were waiting for them. Alex went next, followed by Savachia. Emma paused before ducking into the light.

"Are you sure you two will be okay?" asked Emma.

"Of course, of course," said Neil. "We'll have Gertie seaworthy in no time. Once we get back to the city, we'll tell Derren Fallow where you've gone and send help. Trust us."

"I always have," said Emma, placing her hand on the box. She stepped into the gateway.

"This doesn't look like Las Vegas," said Alex. "At least not in any book I've read."

"Who leaves a gateway in a junkyard?" asked Emma.

"Someone who didn't want it found," answered Pimawa as he stepped over the clown's lips, searching for a stable foothold. "I'd say we get down from here quickly and safely." He held out his hand for Emma, who took it and carefully traipsed her way out of the clown's mouth using the jutting bumpers and rusted neon signs as steps. Alex followed cautiously at a distance.

Savachia jumped down nimbly like a monkey on a rusty jungle gym.

Emma was almost at the bottom when a low rumble stirred beneath her feet. Savachia reached up, sweeping her

WHERE ARE WE?
I THINK WE'RE IN LAS VEGAS.
WHO BLEW IT UP?

off the junk pile into his arms. Behind her, an avalanche of trash came crumbling down, nearly sweeping her with it. She blushed. "Thanks."

"My pleasure," said Savachia. He turned to Alex, who'd gotten down safely on his own. "Did fate happen to send you a map?"

Alex was getting a little tired of all the jibes and jokes about fate. But he had to admit that maybe, this time, Savachia had a point. The gateway was supposed to take them to Awen . . . but how could a junkyard lead them to the jungle girl?

Pimawa squeezed his arm. "I'm sure Awen's close."

Frustrated, Alex kicked a tower of junk. "I just . . . It should be obvious! Maybe they left a trail."

"Or maybe we're not in the right place at all," Savachia said. "Neil did say that gateway probably had several destinations programmed in. Maybe we're just in the wrong one. Face it, those high-tech kidnappers aren't operating out of a junkyard."

Alex kicked the pile of junk again. This time it groaned ominously.

"Can we please get out of here?" asked Emma. "Vegas is full of magicians, right? It shouldn't be hard to find help."

"Maybe, maybe not," said Pimawa. "Vegas attracted performers, but not all of them are actual magicians. Most of them have never heard of the Conjurian."

"Oh, great. We're on our own," grumbled Savachia. "Maybe we can hang signs around town. 'Lost: immortal, jungle girl. If found please contact the talking rabbit.'"

Emma swatted Savachia's shoulder.

"The outpost," said Pimawa. "We have to find the outpost."

"Oh," said Savachia. "Is that all? I should've thought of that. What's an outpost?"

"The Circle set up outposts everywhere in the Flatworld," said Pimawa. "It was a way to keep tabs on anyone who might harm the Conjurian. Especially non-magical magicians who started digging for more secrets."

"Magicians spying on non-magical magicians to keep a

secret magical world that's losing its magic safe." Savachia shook his head. "Makes perfect sense."

"Great!" said Emma. She seemed happy to have a destination. "Where's the outpost?"

"I don't know," said Pimawa. "It's secret."

Savachia threw up his arms. "We can't even find our way out of a junkyard!"

Alex had been scanning his surroundings for some kind of indicator. It would be there. He'd find it. "Listen, all of you. Fate brou—"

"If you finish that sentence, I am going to bury you in junk," Emma said shortly. "Let's go this way."

Alex didn't argue. One way was as good as another, he figured, until he found the clue he was looking for. They moved off, rounding pile after pile of plastic bags and heaps of bricks and tangles of who-knows-what. The sun turned every hunk of metal into a radiator, and the air vibrated with heat.

After the twelfth turn, something twinkled off to the left of Alex's vision. Was that a sign? It must have been. "Over here!" Alex took off around a pile of rusted stoves and broken furniture. "I'm sure of it!"

The glinting thing flashed and jingled, and Alex left the others farther behind in his haste. Turning a corner, Alex was confronted with a heap of black fur in his path, two small metal tags attached to a leather thong looped around its neck.

Alex skidded to a halt, backpedaling in his tracks.

"Not a sign! Not a sign!" he shouted at the others. "It was a dog collar! Run!"

Not just one dog, but two, tore around the pile of rusty stoves after Alex, spit flying from their floppy jowls.

"Oh, absolutely not!" Savachia, kicking up dust, took off.

"Hey! Wait up!" Emma yelled after him.

But the piles of debris made navigating difficult. Savachia went one way, and Emma, Alex, and Pimawa, the other.

The dogs stayed with the larger group of targets, ignoring Savachia completely in favor of the other three. Alex risked a glance over his shoulder, tripped over a scrap of cable poking up out of the dirt, and sprawled headlong. Emma and Pimawa whipped him off his feet, scurrying around a bend.

"Where's Savachia?" gasped Emma.

"Saving himself," grunted Alex, getting his balance once more and shaking their hands off his arms.

They swerved around a corner. Emma grabbed a rusted barrel and flung it behind them. The dogs vaulted it with joyful snarls, and the next second, Alex felt himself falling again as something grabbed the hem of his jeans.

Alex's chin scraped the ground, and he tasted a mouthful of dirt. He braced himself, waiting for the snarling teeth to bite. Then something white flashed next to his head, and one of Pimawa's wide, flat feet thundered into the dog's side, launching it like a cannonball.

A voice called from the right. "Over here! Quick!"

Alex jumped to his feet. He, Pimawa, and Emma scrambled around a rusted, towering cowboy boot and found Savachia balanced on top of a splintered wooden sign he had propped up against a chain-link fence. FREE SLOTS! it read.

Alex felt guilty for doubting Savachia. He raced for the exit ramp the other boy had just provided, with his sister and Pimawa close behind.

Emma was up and over in a flash, turning to help Pimawa, whose paw was already outstretched. Savachia grabbed hold of Alex's hand, and Alex leaped onto the sign.

The rotten wood splintered under his foot, and the dogs bounded toward him. But Alex knew that fate hadn't led him here to become a dog's dinner. He hoped so, anyway. He yanked at his foot. It didn't move. Please, don't let him be wrong about what fate had in store. . . .

All at once, the dogs stopped. They cowered at the base of the ramp, sniffing the air. Then, with a high-pitched whimper and tails tucked, they bolted off into the jungle of metal scraps.

It was several seconds before Alex exhaled.

"What was that?" asked Emma from the other side of the fence, her fingers gripping the wire.

Savachia helped Alex get his foot free, watching for the dogs' return. "It would appear fate might actually be watching out for your klutzy brother after all."

Savachia pushed Alex up the ramp and followed. Emma helped both boys down, and Alex looked around.

They were on a dusty patch of bare ground, with a gravel road nearby. "Which way to the outpost, Pim?" asked Alex, glad his legs had stopped shaking.

"We'll follow the road that way." Pimawa pointed in the direction that led toward the glinting buildings in the distance.

"Um, Pimawa." Emma stopped short.

"Emma, we don't have time—" started Alex.

"Oh." Savachia halted next to Emma, eyeing the Jimjarian.

"Is there another dog?" Pimawa jumped around in a semicircle until he noticed all three of his companions staring at him. Then, as if reading their minds, he looked down at his ragged jacket. "I suppose we should clean up a little first."

"Oooooor," said Savachia, "you should turn into a rabbit. Unless you want to end up in some Vegas sideshow."

"I'm sorry, Pim," agreed Emma. "But you do stand out a bit."

"Right, yes, of course," said Pimawa. "It's been a while."

"How does it work, Pim?" asked Alex. "The whole transmorphing thing? Does it hurt?"

"Not at all," said Pimawa, shaking his head and arms.

"Just be a second. I'll still be able to talk. If someone wouldn't mind grabbing my jacket once I'm done."

"Wait!" said Emma. "You mean you could've talked to us all those years at Mordo's?"

Savachia rolled his eyes. "Sure, a talking rabbit. That wouldn't have scarred you two for life or anything."

In a flash, Pimawa's jacket crumpled to the ground. A twitching white face poked out. "Sorry, Miss Emma, strictly against the rules," said the chubby white rabbit.

"Not sure why this is weirder than him walking on two feet and talking," muttered Alex.

Emma scooped up Pimawa, smiling. "I don't care what shape you take, Pim. I'll always love you. Alex, grab his jacket."

Alex snatched the jacket up, and they hurried down the dusty road toward the sound of traffic and the smell of hot asphalt.

CHAPTER 11

EMMA

The sun rose higher and the air grew hotter as Emma and the others emerged from a stand of scruffy trees behind a pawnshop that had seen better days. Far down the street to their left, glinting casinos competed with the bright sun. They moved cautiously into the shaded alley alongside the pawnshop. All three kids sighed and sat down against the cool stucco walls.

"So now what?" asked Emma. No one answered, and she knew why—because they were all thinking the same thing. They were lost in an alien city with no idea where the outpost was, or if it even existed.

"We don't know where we are. We don't know anyone here," said Emma. "We don't even have money for food or water."

They all licked their lips when she said *water.*

"Where to from here, O wise sage of the fates?" Savachia nodded at Alex.

"We escaped the junkyard, didn't we?" said Alex.

"I guess we did," said Savachia. He glanced sideways at Alex. "Maybe there is something to this fate-protecting-us stuff after all. But could you put in a request that fate hire a limo to take us where we need to go?"

Pimawa hopped to the opening of the alley, sniffing and twisting his ears.

"Come look!" said Pimawa. "You will not believe this!"

Savachia turned to Emma. "Not going to lie, a tiny talking rabbit creeps me out a bit."

Emma couldn't help but giggle as she pushed herself off the cool ground. Savachia and Alex followed. Pimawa jittered at their feet, pointing with his paw across the street.

"Look!" squeaked Pimawa.

They looked. All they saw was an old building, designed to look like a Chinese temple. It was a small, forgotten casino. The flaking sign barely proclaimed:

A neon light bulb pierced by a lightning bolt dangled awkwardly under the sign.

"Bit early for a show," said Emma, scratching Pimawa's ears.

"Yeah," said Savachia. "Wait till we get downtown. Go see something worthwhile, like Cirque du Shadows or something."

Pimawa scrambled up Emma's leg and reached a perch on her shoulder. His fur tickled her cheek. "Mister Electric is the stage name of Marvin Roy! He was a friend of Master Mordo's! He can help us. He might even know the location of the outpost."

Slinging his bag over his shoulder, Alex stepped out of the alley. "This is a sign! Literally and figuratively."

"Alex," said Emma. "The place is probably closed."

"Condemned, more likely," said Savachia.

Alex wrinkled his nose. "Really? We escaped two mutant dogs, who mysteriously decided not to eat us, and then sat down for a rest right in front of one of Uncle Mordo's old buddies? And you guys still don't think fate has something in store for us?"

"Good point," said Savachia.

"Thank you," said Alex.

"Fine," said Emma. She sighed. It was up to her to be the cautious one yet again. "But let's not go racing in there. We'll be careful. Who knows if we can trust this guy, if he's even around."

They headed across the empty road. The silence was creeping Emma out. But then she thought about what Alex had said. They'd gotten out of the junkyard without becoming dog food, it was true. And she had to admit, stumbling across a friend of Uncle Mordo's seemed much more than a coincidence. Emma relaxed a little. Maybe the worst was behind them.

As they reached the opposite sidewalk, a man in a blue suit exited the café on the corner. He had a coffee in one hand, and his phone in the other, and he never glanced once at the three kids and a rabbit heading toward him. As he passed, Savachia nudged Alex into the man's path, and Alex's shoulder brushed the arm holding the coffee cup. The stranger did a half turn, trying not to spill the hot beverage.

"Watch where you're going," snapped the man before returning to his phone.

"Sorry," said Alex. "Why'd you do that?" He swung a half-hearted fist at Savachia, who easily dodged the punch.

"We needed money." Savachia walked backward, shaking a brown leather wallet over Alex's head. "You make a great accomplice."

"You stole his wallet?" shouted Emma.

Savachia's finger shot up to his lips. All three of them looked back to see if the man had heard. Nope. Head down, he was crossing the street a block away.

"You'll get us arrested," protested Emma.

"That is the least of our problems," said Savachia, fishing cash and a credit card out of the wallet. "Now we've got money, and we know somebody in this town. Or at least Pimawa knows someone." He tossed the wallet in a trash can. "Besides, even if we did get arrested, let's face it—we'd be a lot safer behind bars."

They reached the Shanghai Spectral. Savachia held the door for Alex and Emma as Pimawa scooted ahead through their legs.

The inside was shockingly dim. It smelled of old smoke and dust and was a little cooler but not much. The air-conditioning units were losing their battle against the desert heat.

And it was eerily empty. The only noises were the clicking bells and chimes from a bank of slot machines off to their right.

"This is nasty. Looks like they painted the walls with unicorn vomit," said Alex.

But the kids' eyes lit up at the sight of a glass case full of candies and chocolates.

"Right, snack time, then back to finding Tarzan's niece," said Savachia, waving a wad of bills. "It's on me."

Alex slapped a tarnished bell on the counter, letting off a sad, tinny ding. A moment later, a woman emerged from a door behind the counter. She wore a faded red apron and had red hair streaked with gray pulled into a small bun at the back of her head.

"Welcome to the Shanghai Spectral," said the woman. "What can I get you?"

"Three grape sodas and a bag of your finest sautéed corn kernels," said Savachia, peeling off a twenty-dollar bill.

"Sautéed wha—" The woman glanced over her shoulder at the handwritten menu board.

"Popcorn, ma'am," explained Savachia. "Three grape sodas and a popcorn. Please."

"You know you aren't allowed in the casino section," the woman told them, shoveling a scoop of not-so-fresh popcorn into a bag.

"We're here to see Mr. Electric," said Emma.

The woman looked suspiciously at them, sliding the bag of popcorn across the counter.

"He's a friend of our uncle," said Emma. "Have you heard of Mord— Ow!" Emma glared at the rabbit, who'd just nipped her leg. Pimawa shook his head from side to side. Emma bent down and picked him up, hugging him close. "Right, yeah, is Mr. Electric around?"

"Smooth, Em," sighed Alex under his breath.

The woman snapped plastic lids on the sodas, still giving them a doubtful look. She took the twenty dollars and made change, handing a five to Savachia. Then she pointed at double doors just to the other side of the concession stand. "No one sees Mr. Electric without proving themselves first."

"Proving themselves?" Savachia eyed her warily.

"Exactly." The woman leaned across the counter. "You three clearly aren't here for our fine dining, and you're much too nervous to have any interest in a magic show. So that can only mean one thing: you're Conjurian yourselves."

Emma instinctually gripped Pimawa tighter to her chest, and the lady grinned.

"I thought so. If you have any interest in seeing Mr. Electric, you gotta get through me first. So. Prove yourself."

"Um," said Emma. "We aren't exactly . . ." Her voice trailed off. She couldn't do any magic at all—and although Alex had saved her and a lot of other Conjurians by activating the Eye, he had no idea how he'd done it and had never been able to do it again. Anyway, they didn't have the Eye. They'd left it with Derren. Which meant they could do nothing.

"No problem!" Savachia beamed at both the woman and

Emma. He reached into his pocket and pulled out a deck.

"No, no, no. I don't need a simple card trick, boy." The woman waved him off. "Any simpleton off the Strip can do that. I want *magic*. Tell me who I'm thinking of," said the woman, "or leave."

Emma felt her heart sink. "Please. Let me explain—"

Savachia didn't let Emma finish. "Come on. Let's go," he said, pulling on Alex's arm. "We'll find another way."

Alex shook free. "But destiny led us here," he said stubbornly.

"Well, destiny screwed up, then," Savachia said. "Come on, you guys, let's—"

"Your aunt," said Emma suddenly, concentrating hard on the woman behind the counter.

Savachia and Alex turned to stare at her. They looked as surprised as she felt.

She'd heard the words come out of her own mouth with astonishment. She hadn't meant to say that. She hadn't known she was *going* to say it . . . and yet she found herself saying even more.

"She was sick . . . and there was money trouble before she died . . . and now you're thinking of a man. He came and helped."

The woman held Emma's gaze and snorted. "Another cold reader. Get out of here!"

"Wait, no!" Emma continued, "She—she says everything is much better now." The words kept coming. Emma couldn't stop them. "Something about a man—or a pet? A man with a pet. Uncle Reedus and Bo-bo." Like a cold stream flowing through her mind, the visions poured into Emma's head. A woman she'd never seen before, in a ragged sweater, and a man behind her, tall and bearded, with a parrot on his shoulder. Bo-bo the parrot. Whoa. Where had these images in her brain come from?

The aunt and Uncle Reedus and the parrot faded away. Emma saw the woman behind the counter staring at her with both astonishment and respect, and she knew that whatever she'd said, it had been right.

But there was no time to feel relief, because a new image was forming in her mind.

Two figures, a man and a woman—but not the same ones as before. Not the cashier's aunt and uncle. These two looked distant and foggy, colorless. Their sad, gaunt faces turned away from Emma.

Mom? Dad?

The woman smacked a hand down on the counter, and the vision of Emma's parents swirled away, as if poured down a drain. She was back in the casino, staring at the redheaded woman's wide-eyed face.

"Hot dog! You have abilities!" she said, eerily excited. "Good to see some magic still exists in the world. Mr. Electric will see you now. The theater is right through those doors." She tilted her head at the double doors behind the kids and turned to straighten out the candy display.

"Great," said Savachia, grabbing his popcorn and soda. Emma and Alex snatched their drinks, and all three rushed through the theater doors before the woman could change her mind.

"His next show is not until five o'clock!" shouted the woman.

The theater was much darker than the lobby, lit by sickly yellow floor lights lining the aisle. Emma blinked, adjusting to the murk. There were probably enough seats for an audience of two hundred, but no one sat here now. The smell of decaying leather and rotten wood made her crinkle her nose.

"Okay, talk," Savachia said, turning to Emma. "How'd you do that? How'd you know about the aunt? And Uncle Reedus and Bo-bo?"

"Yeah, Em," Alex said. "That was . . . kind of weird."

"I don't know," Emma mumbled. "It was just . . . a coincidence."

She didn't want to think about it. Surely she hadn't actually had a vision of a stranger's dead aunt! And her uncle and his parrot! It was unbelievable. It was *impossible*.

It was nothing more than a coincidence. It had to be because there had been the second vision—the one of her mother and father. And if the woman's aunt and uncle were dead . . . not to mention Bo-bo the parrot . . . then that would mean Mom and Dad were . . .

"There's no such thing as coincidences," Alex asserted, breaking Emma from her thoughts.

"I don't want to talk about it now," she said shortly.

Pimawa wiggled from Emma's arms and jumped to the floor. He hopped toward the stage, where a hunched figure had just emerged from the wings. An old man, wearing a tuxedo that had probably fit him perfectly forty years ago, shuffled around a small table.

Emma took advantage of the distraction. "Is that him?" she whispered.

"I think so," said Alex, giving her one more odd look but dropping the topic of her vision. "There's no one else here."

Emma felt suddenly vulnerable. Could they trust this guy? How well had Uncle Mordo known him?

Suddenly the theater erupted with light. Emma, Alex, and Savachia dove behind the first row of chairs. Onstage, the old man held a balloon-sized light bulb in his bare hand. The bulb burned brighter and brighter, like a small sun.

"Wow!" Alex peeked over the chair, shielding his eyes. "Does he still have powers?"

Before Pimawa could answer, the giant bulb hissed, then shattered, restoring the darkness.

"Ow!" shouted Mr. Electric, rubbing his hand. "Dang nabbered batteries overheated again!" He pushed his jacket out of the way, revealing a black box clipped to his waistline. He opened the box, fiddling with the wires inside. "Aaaack! It's fried. Right, let's move on, then."

Mr. Electric placed the broken bulb on the table and picked up two glass rings. One lit up red, the other blue. With a few well-practiced moves, he linked the rings. The two solid circles were now joined. With slow grace, he pulled the rings apart—or he tried to. *Tink!* They remained joined. He repeated the process, each time pulling harder. "Oh, for Pete's sake," shouted Mr. Electric. He yanked the rings. *Clank! Clank! Clank!* In a fit of rage, he hurled the props offstage.

Emma watched the rings roll past. When she looked back, Alex was halfway up the stairs.

"Excuse me," said Alex.

"Who—who's there?" Mr. Electric snatched up the jagged bulb. "Show yourself!"

Savachia vaulted onto the stage, placing himself between Alex and the old man. He held both hands open as Mr. Electric waved his improvised weapon. "Easy there, Gramps. Don't light me up."

Emma joined them, pulling Alex back to a safe distance. He jerked free, sidestepping Savachia. "It's okay. Mordo the Mystifier sent us," said Alex. "We need to find the outpost, you know, the one that sends info back to the Conjurian."

Mr. Electric's face pinched quizzically.

"We're supposed to meet with you," Alex said earnestly. "Can you tell us where the outpost is?"

Shaking his head, Mr. Electric focused on Alex. "Mordo sent you?" His brow creased, shadowing his sunken eyes with suspicion. "How do you know Mordo?"

That was when Pimawa hopped onto the table and addressed the old man. "Hello, Master Roy."

The old man dropped the bulb. His eyes widened. "Pimawa? Is that you!" He sprung forward, wrapping the rabbit in his arms. "Oh, my dear boy. So good to see you!"

Pimawa bowed his head as the old man nuzzled his neck. "Greetings, Master Roy. It's good to see you again. I apologize for the circumstances. Allow me to introduce—"

Mr. Electric's eyes lit up. "Alex and Emma Maskelyne! As I live and breathe. The spitting image of your parents. My, I

remember . . ." His voice trailed off. "Oh, my dear children, I am so sorry."

Mr. Electric took Emma's hand in his. "Your parents. I did not know them well, but I helped them out a couple times."

"Really?" asked Alex. Emma saw that he'd gotten busy examining the apparatus on the table. "You were an agent of M.A.G.E. too?"

"Oh, ha!" Marvin chuckled. He released Emma's hand. "No. Nothing like that. They came to me once, asking an odd question. They wanted to know if they could travel through a gateway to a destination without another gateway on the other end."

"That's not possible, though, is it?" asked Alex.

"Your parents hoped my engineering abilities would uncover a way," said Mr. Electric. "I researched and experimented for months. The last time I saw them, I had to tell them I had failed. Such sweet folks. I thought they'd be crushed. Didn't dampen their spirits in the least. In fact, they told me they'd managed it themselves."

"How?" asked Emma.

Mr. Electric shook his balding head. "I never found out."

Emma took the old man's hand this time.

"Mr. Roy, we believe our parents are alive." Or at least Emma continued to hope as much. "If you could remember anything at all, it might help us find them. Did they mention where they were trying to go?"

"We already know where they were trying to go," said Alex, tapping the book inside the cloth sack.

"Hush, Alex," Emma said scornfully. "Blackstone's not a real place."

Alex shook his head at her, his jaw set stubbornly. "But you can tell us where the outpost is, right?" he asked Mr. Electric. "You've got to know."

The old man looked alarmed at the mention of Blackstone. "Not smart. Not smart at all. Go back while you can—now." He ushered Alex and Emma toward the stairs. "Hurry. Go before it's too late. Before they know you're here."

"Before who knows we're here?" asked Emma.

"Sanctum," replied Mr. Electric in a harsh whisper.

"Sanctum!" repeated Savachia. "They're the ones who took Awen."

Mr. Electric looked around as if the walls were listening. "Go before they—"

A loud sound echoed outside the theater doors. Boots stomped. Someone barked commands. The doors burst open, and the sepia light from the lobby outlined the forms of armored soldiers.

"—find you," finished Mr. Electric. "Too late!"

CHAPTER 12

ALEX

Alex stared at the platoon of armored soldiers who rushed into the theater, heading down the aisle. Each carried a long black rod, the end hissing and sparking.

"Mr. Electric!" Alex yanked the man's sleeve, spinning him halfway around. "Where is the outpost?"

"No time!" Mr. Electric shoved the kids toward the rear of the stage. "Out the back. Turn right. There's an emergency exit at the end of the hall. Quickly!"

"Let's go, little man," said Savachia, grabbing Alex under one armpit. "Gramps is right. We gotta get out of here."

Alex tried breaking free. This was wrong! Fate had brought them here to find the outpost—they couldn't leave

without that information! As Savachia dragged him backward, he saw the men leap on the stage. Mr. Electric snatched a bulb off the table and held it out, as threateningly as he could, toward the soldiers.

That seemed pointless, thought Alex. Then the bulb flared, brighter and brighter. The soldiers cringed, shielding their faces. And that was the last Alex saw of Mr. Electric, the man who had the answer they needed.

Savachia yanked Alex behind the heavy curtain, cutting off the solar flare coming from the stage. Pimawa led the way backstage, into a wing and then down a hallway, where they could just make out the faint glow of the Exit sign through the dust-laden air.

"There it is!" said Savachia. "C'mon!"

The kids caught up to Pimawa, already thumping a foot anxiously against the dented metal door. Emma pushed at the crash bar. The door remained closed. Savachia jumped in to help. They battered at the mechanism. It didn't budge.

At the other end of the hall, six guards charged around the corner, their electric batons at the ready.

Alex looked around for another way out. He searched for a weapon. There had to be something! A sign, any indication of what to do!

The guards slowed down, as if they knew their targets had no way out. The lead soldier scraped her baton along the wall, releasing blue sparks that reflected off her spiked red hair.

"What now, fate boy?" Savachia threw his shoulder into the door again and again. "Are we supposed to

escape or get tased into submission by these sci-fi-movie rejects?"

Honestly, Alex didn't know what was next. He thought back to the junkyard and the dogs retreating at the last second for no reason. Would another miracle save them now? Or had that been dumb luck? No, they would never have made it this far on luck. He was sure of that.

He just wasn't sure what was about to happen next.

Then a rafter creaked over their heads.

Everyone looked up. The soldiers, Alex, Emma, Savachia, and Pimawa—all wore the same horrified expression. A few feet above their heads, crouching on the metal support beam, an enormous white tiger roared.

"How's that for a sign?" asked Alex, staring in awe at the furry miracle that was busy thrashing the guards.

"I, for one," sputtered Savachia, "did not see that coming."

The tiger roared, swinging its talons. The Sanctum soldiers scrambled over one another, running back toward the stage.

"Hey!" yelled Emma. "Getting stuck in a hallway with a tiger is not an escape plan! Help me with the door!"

Both Alex and Savachia joined Emma, ramming the door

again and again. Alex pushed his back into the door. Legs burning, he watched the guards flee, their shredded armor dangling. The tiger did not give chase. It pivoted instead, its green eyes targeting the kids banging on the door.

Alex redoubled his efforts when he saw the giant cat stalking toward them.

"This is some sort of sick joke!" Savachia screamed right in the big cat's face.

"What are you doing?" Emma gasped.

"I don't know!" said Savachia. "Aren't you supposed to scare them off or something? Ask your brother! He's the one with the direct helpline."

The cat, a few feet away, pulled back its lips to reveal ivory teeth and let out a low growl that vibrated the walls. All three kids pressed up against the door. Alex felt his shoulder blade press into something sharp and uncomfortable but didn't dare move.

A squeak erupted from ground level, and a white blur leaped past Alex's knees right at the tiger. Alex twitched, felt the thing that was digging into his shoulder give way, and realized that it must have been some sort of switch as the door suddenly swung open, spilling all three kids onto the hard pavement. The door slammed shut behind them.

Alex propped himself up and shook his sore head. The hot air was a welcome relief compared to tiger breath. Groaning, Savachia and Emma got to their knees, preparing to run for their lives.

"Pimawa!" Emma yelled. The only answer was a great

hissing sound from behind the closed door, followed by an angry growl. She scrambled for the handle, but Savachia grabbed her arm, stopping her.

"He sacrificed himself to give us time to get away," said Savachia. "Don't let his sacrifice be in vain."

Alex could see that Emma was ready to argue. He grabbed at her arm too. "Em, don't. Look at that." He turned his sister around to see the thing he was staring at.

The exit had dumped them into a wide alleyway between two buildings. To his left, at one end of the alley, Alex could see a parking lot. To his right was a chain-link fence, partially trampled as if something large and powerful had jumped on it. Alex had a good idea what had done the damage.

The crumpled fence exposed an abandoned gas station where a rusted van sat idling. Alex wondered for an instant whether the tiger had jumped from the back of the van or whether it had eaten the driver. The thought slipped out of his head when a striking man rolled into view around the far side of the vehicle.

He was bald, covered in what looked like a mass of samples from a fabric store, and sitting in a wheelchair gilded with chrome and jewels.

EMMA

The man in the wheelchair didn't seem too surprised to see three disheveled children in an alley behind an old theater. "Get in the van," he said calmly. He waved them toward the broken fence.

"But Pimawa's in there!" Emma shook Savachia's hand off her arm and grabbed at the handle of the door.

"So is an eight-hundred-pound man-eater!" said Savachia, pulling her back again. "Emma, there's nothing we can do for him."

The strength drained from Emma's grip. Savachia was right. What could she do? Rush back in and get devoured too? She turned away from the door.

Pimawa was gone. He'd followed her in that theater just like the Conjurians and Jimjarians had followed her into battle . . . and now he was dead.

Just like Mom and Dad. Emma blinked away tears and saw her brother climbing over the toppled fence.

"Alex, get back here!" Emma yelled. What was her little brother doing now? "Who's that?" she asked, staring at the man in the wheelchair.

"A random dude in an alley, that's who." Savachia pulled Emma away from the stranger, toward the parking lot. "C'mon, we'll hot-wire a car and get out of here."

"No time for introductions," said the man. "Get in the van now."

Alex cleared the fence and jumped to the ground beside the wheelchair. "I'm going in the van," he said, nodding at the newcomer.

"Alex, stop this!" Emma wanted to scream.

"For crying out loud." Alex shook his head. "How could it be more obvious that we are supposed to go this way?"

Savachia jogged away toward the parking lot. Emma spun to stare at his back. She couldn't blame him for not wanting to get in a stranger's van, but he wasn't going to leave them . . . was he?

“We have to stick together,” she pleaded. Savachia slowed and stopped. Emma felt a surge of relief that was ruined when a black truck screeched to a halt, blocking the other end of the alley.

Armed Sanctum troops spilled out of the van. Savachia quickly retraced his steps.

“On second thought,” said Savachia, grabbing Emma and helping her over the jiggling fence, “maybe we should give your brother the benefit of the doubt.”

As she sprinted to the van, Emma looked back, hoping beyond hope that somehow Pimawa would materialize. But she saw nothing of the white rabbit, and all she could hear was the sound of clomping boots and the sizzle from the black batons as the troopers tramped toward the fence.

"Move faster," shouted the man in the wheelchair. He was already sliding the chair onto a lift that raised him into the driver's seat.

Alex was inside as well, reaching an arm out the van door. "C'mon, c'mon!"

Emma threw herself into the back of the vehicle. But Savachia wasn't beside her. She rolled over, sat up, and stared at the Sanctum soldiers next to the fence, raising their sparking batons, and, in their grasp, Savachia.

"Go! Go!" Savachia yelled. He kicked against his captors, but there was no getting loose.

"Hang on," said their mysterious new driver.

"Savachia!" Emma cried out.

Five of the soldiers sprinted toward the front of the van. The rest formed a line, closing in on the back.

Emma zeroed in on the angry, buzzing ends of the batons, wondering how unpleasant it would be when they contacted her skin. Savachia hung limply in the guards' hands, no longer struggling.

The guard nearest the driver's window was the one with spiked red hair that glinted in the sun. She smacked her baton against the van. "Toss the keys out of the window and come out with your hands on your head," she ordered.

"Alex, what are we going to do?" Emma gripped her brother's hand.

A thunderous crash came from the alley. The emergency exit door exploded off its hinges, clattering against the alley wall, and the white tiger cleared the fence in one bound, sprinting toward the van.

CHAPTER 13

ALEX

The stink of melting rubber and hot sand filled the van as it rocketed forward, away from the Sanctum soldiers. Alex didn't even notice. His eyes were locked on the monstrous predator and the limp bunny hanging from its maw.

Alex crept toward the beast.

"Alex!" warned Emma. "Don't make any sudden movements."

"Calm down," said Alex. "She's not going to eat us."

Alex waited for the snarky retort from Savachia before remembering it wasn't going to come. How much more could they lose? Alex thought. Fate had brought them here, to this van . . . so it had to be the right place. But he'd never thought fate would sacrifice Savachia and Pimawa along the way.

Carefully, Alex reached out toward the tiger. The massive animal watched him with what Alex would have sworn was mild amusement.

The van jolted. Alex crashed backward. The tiger's jaws opened. The little white rabbit jerked to life, hopping off the cat's paw and into Emma's arms.

"Pim! You're okay!" Emma squeezed the rabbit, turning, shielding him from the tiger.

The tiger shook its head, licking its jowls as if ridding its mouth of a bad taste. It hunched forward, and its moist breath puffed at the kids' hair. Its claws made a jaw-tingling screech across the metal floor. Lips pulled up, revealing teeth whiter than its fur. Emma yelped, and the van skidded to a halt.

"I am Raymond Ludwig," said their driver. Concentrating so hard on the tiger, Alex had almost forgotten that there was anyone driving the van at all.

The man turned to glance at them over his shoulder and seemed to be watching their faces to see if they recognized the name at all. "Ludwig and Fischbacher?" he prompted. His eyes flashed over to the tiger, then back to their panicked faces. "Yes, well, Raisha always stole the show." He turned back to the road as the streetlight ahead turned green, and

the van jolted into motion once again.

"Raisha, if you would, please."

The tiger swung her head up and back. Her body trembled. She arched forward, clamping the crumpled sheet in her mouth, and spun in a circle, draping the cloth over her body.

"Your clothes, my dear." Ludwig tossed a bundle from the passenger seat into the back of the van.

The sheet writhed and twitched. There were a couple of loud roars, and then it was still. The shape underneath the sheet was still large, but not as bulky as the tiger. A furry white hand reached out and pulled the clothes under the sheet. A little more rustling, then the sheet dropped.

"Whooooa," leaked from Alex's lips. "You're a Wograth!"

He'd seen beings like Raisha before, in the carvings that filled Awen's hut. Raisha's face was still tiger-ish, except less

furry. She had long flowing white hair and a nubby horn on each side of her forehead. The sheet dropped, revealing a human body with more fur than most humans had. She wore a vest and loose pants that stopped above her calves.

Pimawa squirmed in Emma's arms. His body shifted, morphing into his bipedal form.

"Ah! Pimawa! Get off!" shouted Emma, pinned to the van floor.

But Pimawa ignored her. Panicked, he yanked on the handle of the van's door.

Alex grabbed his wrists. "Pimawa, be careful! Tumbling out of a van going eighty is not going to end well!"

Pimawa crumpled into the back corner, which at least

allowed Emma to sit up. His eyes seemed unable to look away from the childhood nightmare only three feet away.

Without warning, Ludwig stomped on the brake. Alex pitched forward, headbutting Raisha in her furry stomach. The Wograth lifted him up, sniffing. Her lips flared as she ran her long, thick fingernails along Alex's neck.

"Right, then." Ludwig craned around, looking sternly at his passengers. "You've never heard of Ludwig and Fischbacher? Who sent you?"

Raisha, eyes filled with suspicion, wrapped her paw around Alex's neck.

"Hey! Hold on! You're the one who came for us," said Emma.

"Of course we did," said Ludwig. "We were patrolling the junkyard when Raisha caught your scent."

"Wait," said Alex, eyeing Raisha nervously. Fate hadn't brought him here to be eaten by a were-tiger, he knew—but those fingernails really were quite sharp. "*She's* the one that scared off the dogs?"

Raisha uttered a low growl.

"Of course," said Ludwig. "Raisha followed you to be sure. Then you ran off into that dumpy casino. When I saw the Sanctum goons arrive, I thought for sure you were our replacements."

"Replacements for what?" asked Emma.

"For the outpost," said Ludwig. His gaze moved to the side window. "But I seem to be mistaken. You have never heard of us, so I assume you are not here to relieve us." He sighed. "Which brings me back to my initial question. Who sent you?"

Raisha's claws tightened on Alex's neck. He grinned at her. She sniffed him again. "You do not fear me?" she inquired.

"No," said Alex. His smile widened. "We were meant to find you."

"Find us for what?" asked Ludwig.

"We need your help," said Emma. "Sanctum kidnapped our friend—and a girl we know too. We have to rescue both of them. We need the girl to find—to find our parents." Her voice wobbled, and Alex gave her a curious look. What was up with her?

"Who are your parents?" asked Ludwig.

Pimawa seemed to regain a droplet of courage. "Henry and Evelynne Maskelyne."

"Who?" asked Ludwig.

As if he'd forgotten the Wograth's presence for a moment, Pimawa shot up, his ears bent against the roof. "It seems we should be the ones affronted! These children are Alex and Emma Maskelyne. Vanquishers of the Shadow Conjurer!"

Ludwig considered this for a moment, exchanging a look with Raisha. "You must forgive us. We have heard little from the Conjurian. There were rumors of this Shadow Conjurer kidnapping magicians. Master Agglar had given us orders to be on the lookout. However, our schedule was overflowing with other issues."

"The Sanctum?" guessed Emma.

"Yes," said Ludwig. "It seems we have a common foe." Ludwig jerked the van into drive. "We can discuss it at the outpost. For now, let's get you out of the open."

The van sped out of the city toward the sandy mountains surrounding Las Vegas.

EMMA

The mountaintop was all rock accented by shaggy brush. A warm wind blew sand into the van when the rear doors creaked opened. Emma saw that the land around was empty save for a lone cement building. Next to that were four concrete supports where a tower had once stood.

Ludwig's chair kicked up almost as much dust as the van as he motored toward the solitary structure. "Hurry, now. Remember, eyes are everywhere these days."

Raisha took up the rear, sniffing the air one last time before she watched Ludwig and the newcomers inside. The last to enter, she closed and locked the door behind her.

Inside, scattered pieces of desks and office chairs crowded the corners, leaving one square dustless area in the middle.

"Trapdoor," said Alex.

Ludwig rolled into the clean space, gesturing for the others to join him. "Perceptive. Everyone scooch in tight. Don't want anyone losing an arm. Not yet, anyway."

Emma hesitated. Things were moving too fast. Sanctum knew they were here. Their soldiers had Savachia. And now she and Alex were at the mercy of two complete strangers, one of whom was a myth to terrify young Jimjarians, no less. And they were going into a mountain hideaway with these people? But what choice did they have? They had to get Savachia back, and these two seemed to have information about Sanctum.

Emma noticed Ludwig smiling at her. There was no sign of malice or ill intent on his face.

"Kidding," said Ludwig. "Let's all get downstairs so you can relax. Food, rest. We can compare notes and see what's what."

Reluctantly, Emma stepped forward and squeezed onto

the clean square of floor next to Alex. She didn't know if she could trust this odd man or not . . . but she knew she couldn't stand being left behind.

Ludwig clicked a carved lion's head on his armrest. With a jarring shudder, the floor sank down. The abandoned office slipped away overhead, replaced by smooth cement walls. Farther down, the walls changed to bare rock. The platform jolted to a halt in a low-ceilinged cave. Ludwig bumped his chair off the platform.

"Right this way," he told them. A spotlight on his chair lit a smooth path through the winding cavern.

"This is awesome," said Alex. "Did you make this?"

Ludwig chuckled. "It was a mob hideout, back when the Mafia ran Las Vegas." His smile withered. "And now it is a hideout for magicians."

The air was wonderfully cooler. Emma was grateful for that. She still wasn't sure if they were doing the right thing or the wrong one, following this stranger. And she was even less sure when a ghost roared out of the darkness.

It was an exact twin of Raisha, except that it was glowing green and blue and swooping at them through the air. Pimawa jerked backward, tripping over Ludwig's chair.

"It's a trap! Back to the lift!" he yelled.

Emma had known it! She should never have let them come down into this cave! They were helpless—and Alex had apparently lost his mind. He stepped calmly forward into the monster's path. It crouched and leaped, clawing the air above his head. Its roar echoed off the stone walls all around.

Then the creature was back in front of Alex once more. It crouched and leaped, clawing the air above his head. Its roar echoed. . . .

Wait. What was going on here?

"A hologram!" said Alex, jabbing his arm into the translucent Wograth.

"Sorry. My apologies," said Ludwig, rolling through the ghost. "Gracious, I had forgotten how startling it is. And, yes, it is a hologram of sorts. Of course you're familiar with Pepper's ghost."

"Pepper's what?" asked Alex.

Ludwig spun, sending a shocked look first at Alex, then at Pimawa. "How is it that the children of magicians have never heard of Pepper's ghost?"

"Alex and Emma are new to the history of magic," said

Pimawa. Then he added snidely, "Also, they were preoccupied with saving the Conjurian."

Raisha snarled. "Manners, Jimjarian."

"It's okay," said Ludwig, patting Raisha's arm. "I think we are all overwhelmed by how little we know these days." He spun his chair back around, motoring a few yards past the hologram to an iron door. "Fisch! Fisch! Turn off the security perimeter and open the door!"

With a snarl, Raisha slipped through the hologram, slashing at its head with her claws.

Alex followed close behind, happily trailing a hand inside the apparition. "It's wet!" he said, and Emma saw his eyes immediately track down the source of the moisture. She followed his gaze and spotted the rectangular box, off to the side, hidden behind a craggy rock. Mist sprayed out through a tube in the front. Below that was a lens.

"This is so cool!" Alex exclaimed. "It uses the water like a movie screen."

"Yes. In the old days, they used angled mirrors. The 'ghosts' were actors hidden below the stage," said Ludwig. "Fisch was the genius who figured out how to use fog. Got quite the response from a packed theater during our show. But that's all well behind us now. Along with the Saw of Death, the Ring of Fire, and the Spirit Cabinet." He nodded at a dark mahogany wardrobe leaning against a wall, etched with intricate patterns and symbols.

"All relics now of a time long gone," Ludwig went on. "Haven't used that beauty since our Fourth of July show."

Alex ran a finger over the wood, trying to puzzle out how it worked. "What was the Fourth of July show?" he asked.

"It was our last show, although we didn't know it," said Ludwig. "My partner and I built a tower of pyrotechnic destruction. Fireworks, flame ball cannons, you name it. Fisch strapped himself to it and had to escape before it went off. We

were expecting to perform it several more times, but, well, we didn't. And so. Yes. Had to store everything somewhere."

The steel door swung open, revealing a man dressed more garishly than Ludwig, which until that point, Emma would have thought impossible. He was tall, solidly built under a one-piece suit strewn with green and blue feathers. His blond hair, which was at least forty years younger than his face, made him look like a lion poised on a hilltop.

He beamed at Ludwig. "The looks on your faces were worth a thousand Van Goghs!"

"Ah, and here's the man now! I'd like to introduce you to my partner, Berol Fischbacher," said Ludwig.

"You can call me Fisch," said Berol Fischbacher. "Or Fischbacher the Fantastic, or cosmic stud muffin, or—"

"How about letting our guests inside?" said Ludwig, rolling through the doorway and clipping Fisch's toe.

Fischbacher swept aside. "Ow! Yes! Welcome! Come in, come in. We are delighted. Honestly, we thought the Circle had forgotten about us."

"They have," said Ludwig.

Fischbacher's smile drooped. "They aren't here to take over?"

"Afraid not," said Ludwig. "May I introduce Alex and Emma Maskelyne, and their Jimjarian companion, Pimawa."

They all shuffled in. Fisch shook each hand enthusiastically.

"Whoa," said Alex. "The mob knew how to live."

They were in a large atrium, topped with a once-copper dome that had turned a vibrant green. Its petal-shaped

windows had been boarded up. The arches all around the atrium were adorned with gothic lanterns, each holding several lit candles, casting a watery gold light.

"We have much to do," said Ludwig. "Have a look around while Raisha scrapes up some refreshments. She makes the best Cuban sandwiches."

Raisha playfully twitched her tail across Ludwig's face as she headed off through one of several arches leading away from the atrium.

They did have a look around. Displayed about the room stood mannequins wearing costumes from Ludwig and Fisch's stage show. There were steel cages and garishly painted boxes and lobby posters.

As they wandered, Alex gave Ludwig a brief retelling of how they'd beaten the Shadow Conjurer. Emma walked out of earshot.

Hearing what had happened back at the Tree of Dedi, even the abridged version, still made her stomach turn. The only thing she could picture was those people who had rushed into battle behind her. They'd nearly died. And now Savachia was gone.

Gone just like her parents. The thought brought back something she'd been trying not to think about—what exactly had happened in the lobby of the Shanghai Spectral? How had she known about the woman's aunt and uncle?

Footsteps shuffled behind her. By the sound, she guessed that Fisch's zebra slippers were making them.

"You know," Fisch began, "I remember the first time I experienced my magic powers. Mind you, like most magicians for the past century, it was nothing breathtaking. I was six when it first happened."

Emma did not feel like talking, least of all to someone she'd only just met. She leaned against an archway, looking at nothing much and hoping Fisch would take the hint.

"Mr. Luwftwig's Pharmacy," continued Fisch. "I saw a pack of gum in that glass cabinet, Big Bubba's Double Chew Gum. Oh, how I wanted that gum! My parents didn't have the money for frivolous treats and such. Every week I went to the pharmacy with my mom to pick up Nana's medicine. I would stare at that gum the entire time Mom stood at the counter."

Emma found herself getting a little interested. She could see the young boy Fisch, staring into the display case, longing. Emma knew about longing.

"Then it happened," Fisch went on. "One day, I stared

and stared, closed my eyes, and visualized the gum in my hand. When I opened my eyes, a pack of Big Bubba's was sitting in my tiny palm. Mr. Luwftwig barked, 'Don't take things out of the display!' It mortified my mother. Got the switch that day. Enough about me, though. What did you see?" asked Fisch.

Emma paused. How on earth could he know? He couldn't be talking about . . . ? "What did I see where?" she asked innocently.

Fisch spun around to face her. "In the casino. You saw, didn't you?"

Her curiosity got the best of her. "How did you know?"

His smile was gentle, understanding. "My dear, I have watched so many magicians have their first magical experience. I knew the second you arrived."

Emma hesitated, looking back at Fisch. She wanted to tell someone. But what if he laughed at her?

Even worse, what if he believed her? Because if he believed her, that might make it true.

Emma wanted to sprint out of the room. Instead she said, "I saw someone's dead aunt. And uncle. And his parrot." No reaction from Fisch. Either he was unimpressed or he knew there was more. "And I . . . I saw . . . my parents."

A stabbing ache bolted through Emma's chest. She waited for Fisch to say she must have been wrong. That she had a vivid imagination. That she'd had a delusion.

He said nothing of the sort. He nodded sadly.

"You've found your power, my dear," he said gently. "It's a hard one to have to bear."

Her power. Her magical power. Her brother could activate the Eye of Dedi . . . and Emma could see the dead. And the dead included her parents.

Fisch opened his arms. Surprising herself, Emma ran to him, soaking his robe with tears.

She had only just met Fisch, but now she was glad she had.

CHAPTER 14

ALEX

Alex was just wrapping up his tale when Emma and Fisch rejoined the group. Raisha entered after them, pushing a squeaky metal cart covered with plates of sandwiches and pastries.

"Wow, you're living large," said Alex.

"We may live in a cave," said Ludwig, wheeling up behind the cart. "But we are far from Neanderthals."

Alex lined up behind Emma, and Raisha handed them each a plate. Pimawa eyed the sandwiches. "You made these?" He glanced briefly at Raisha, his whiskers twitching.

"They are not poisoned, Jimjarian," answered Raisha.

"No feuding," said Fisch, stepping in and loading up Pimawa's plate.

"What do you know about Sanctum?" asked Alex, biting into what had to be the best-tasting thing he had eaten in some time.

Ludwig led the kids and their overflowing plates over to a leather couch.

"As to what we know about Sanctum, not a lot," said Ludwig. "We believe Eleanor Latiff is behind it. An eccentric billionaire. She became increasingly impulsive after her son died, or at least that's what I've heard. She opened the Ka Casino not long after."

"And that's when magicians started disappearing," said Fisch.

"At first," continued Ludwig, "we thought magicians were leaving Vegas because they couldn't compete with the Ka and Angel Xavier. He was their star performer. Almost every night he pulled huge crowds. Then Latiff announced

a psychic challenge. Anyone who could prove they had real psychic abilities, specifically the ability to contact the dead, would win ten million dollars. People came from all over the world. Most of them were never seen again."

Alex swallowed a bite of sandwich. "That makes sense! Angel Xavier was the Shadow Conjurer, so Sanctum and this Latiff lady must have been behind him all this time. He was draining power from magicians in the Conjurian—I bet Latiff was luring in more magicians with her ten-million-dollar prize so she could drain the power from them here too!"

"What's Latiff's goal?" asked Emma. "What does she need all that power for? Angel Xavier was making people into Rag-O-Rocs." She shuddered. "Is that what Latiff's doing too? Or something else?"

"Ah," said Ludwig. "Good question. One that has befuddled us for quite some time. We'd been trying to figure it out, asking questions. Then inspectors showed up at our theater. They made up animal cruelty charges and that was that."

Raisha snarled, half a doughnut protruding from her furry lips.

Fisch rubbed her back. "The theater was our home. Raisha's home. In the blink of an eye, our careers were over. Agglar, bless him, moved us here."

Alex put his plate down, not bothering to wipe the crumbs from his mouth. "Okay, so our next step is clear. We've got to get inside the Ka Casino. That's where Sanctum has its headquarters, right? So that'll be where Awen is. And Savachia too. We've got to get them both back."

Ludwig and Fisch looked nervously at each other.

"I'm afraid that's impossible," said Fisch. "Even for two fabulously retired illusionists."

"Come," said Ludwig. "We'll show you."

Ludwig and Fisch led them across the atrium into a tubular hallway. It wound up and around, ending in a spherical room hewn from the rock. On the far side a squat, high-powered telescope stood in front of a massive iron plate on the wall.

"Cool!" said Alex, rushing forward to check out the telescope. "You guys are into astronomy?"

"Far from it," said Fisch.

Fisch adjusted several large knobs before looking through the telescope's eyepiece. Then he tugged the iron plate in the wall aside. The city of Las Vegas sparkled against a dark horizon. "Have a look."

Alex squished his eye against the eyepiece. Ka Casino filled his vision, a gleaming pyramid shimmering in the sun. But the point of the pyramid had been sliced off, leaving the casino with a flat roof. On it, Alex could make out at least twelve Sanctum guards piecing together what looked like scaffolding.

"They're putting up some kind of platform," said Alex.

"Might I take a look, young Alex?" asked Pimawa, trading places with the boy. "I'm not sure I understand what they are doing."

"It must have something to do with the big show," Fisch said. "There have been signs up all over the city. Angel Xavier is returning to the stage."

Alex and Emma froze, turning to him. "Angel Xavier?" Alex said. Emma shivered.

"Yes."

"But he disappeared. After the battle," Emma said softly. "Did he really come back . . . here?"

"It's possible," Pimawa admitted. He turned from the telescope. "But it does not seem likely."

Alex paced around the room. "If your star is missing, why keep promoting his show?"

"The show must always go on," said Fisch with a sad look at Ludwig and Raisha.

Alex's steps quickened. "Or maybe there's not going to be a show at all! Maybe they're up to something else!" So many

ideas drifted through his head. A billionaire, a dead son, a star magician who'd also been a heinous villain, and a pebble that held the key to all the magic in the world. All these things had to be connected in some way. How?

He paused, looking at Ludwig and Fisch and Raisha. "Our parents were on a quest to unlock the Eye. Angel Xavier was trying to get his hands on it too. So maybe Latiff wants it now. Maybe that's what this is all about."

"What about your friend?" asked Ludwig. "Awen, was it? What does Latiff want her for?"

"She's not exactly a friend," Emma said. "She sort of kidnapped us and everything."

"And I don't know why those Sanctum soldiers grabbed her." Alex's shoulders slumped. He paced again and stopped. "I know how we can find out, though!" He raced out of the room.

"Has your brother suffered any head trauma recently?" asked Fisch. He seemed genuinely concerned.

A moment later, Alex flew back into the observatory with his bag. Huffing, he pulled the ancient book out and handed it Raisha. "This is why fate brought us together!"

Raisha looked at Fisch. Ludwig looked at them both. "What is this?" asked Raisha.

"Alex," said Emma. "I don't know if we should—"

"Trust them?" said Alex. "Emma, it's okay. Think about it. What are the odds of us running into a Wograth? The one person who can translate the book we found at Awen's place? The book with a picture of our parents in it?" He was met with doubtful looks from Emma and Pimawa. "How many more signs do you need? Whatever's in that book will tell us why our parents went to Blackstone." He looked up at Raisha. "You can read it, can't you?"

Raisha opened the book, carefully turning the fragile pages with the tips of her claws. She moved closer to the telescope window, allowing sunlight to cascade over the ancient text. The normally hard lines in her face softened. Her green eyes grew wet with moisture.

Alex slid down on his knees next to Raisha. "Can you tell us what it says?"

Turning her head, Raisha wiped her eyes and her nose. She took a deep purring breath. "It says there was a war. Between Wograths and Jimjarians."

Hearing this, Pimawa's ears twitched up. He stepped closer, eyeing the open book over Raisha's shoulder.

Raisha continued. "Dedi arrived in the middle of the war. He negotiated a peace. The Jimjarians would stay on their island, and the Wograths would retreat to their own home."

"To Blackstone?" Alex asked.

"Yes," Raisha replied. "But it isn't just a place. At least not an ordinary place. Blackstone is . . . What is the right word?" She tapped her clawed hand lightly on her chest. "The heart of magic. The heartland. And that's where Dedi went. He took the Eye with him."

Alex nodded. "So Mom and Dad went to Blackstone, looking for the Eye! Right. That makes sense."

Raisha returned her gaze to the book. "The Wograths

swore to protect both. The Eye and the Conjurian. To keep them safe from all outsiders by making sure they stayed in Blackstone forever."

Unable to contain herself, Emma placed a hand on Raisha's shoulder. "Well, do you know where Blackstone is? Isn't that where you're from?"

"No," said Raisha. "Ludwig and Fisch found me on a trip to Iceland when I was only a cub. I don't have many clear memories of Blackstone. Just a sense that it was—different. A place like no other. But—" She caught herself.

"But what?" asked Emma.

Raisha looked pleadingly at Ludwig, then Fisch.

"What is it?" asked Ludwig. "It's okay, Raisha. We need to learn as much as we can."

The Wograth pushed the book toward Alex. She stood to leave and said, "Even if I did know where it was, it wouldn't help you. The one thing I know is that the Wograths will do anything to keep Blackstone safe. They kill anyone who enters it."

The sound of Raisha's feet padding away seemed to take all the air with her. Suddenly everyone felt the rising heat from the single beam of light penetrating the cave.

Dropping to the ground, Emma rested her folded arms on her knees and buried her face. Anyone who entered Blackstone was as good as dead. Raisha had just said so.

And if Alex was right, and their parents had gone to Blackstone . . .

Then that would explain Emma's vision. Her parents were gone. Dead. Lost to her forever. How was she going to find the words to tell Alex what she now knew was the truth?

Alex rubbed his sister's back. "Em? Em, come on. Don't give up. You can't quit on me now. We've got to find out—"

"Find out what?" Emma lifted her head, turning teary red eyes on her brother. "The stupid secret of the Eye? Don't you see how this ends? Everyone that goes after that big secret dies!"

"Emma, listen," Alex said, his voice soft. "We're so close. We just have to get back the person who has the rest of the answers."

"You mean Awen," said Emma. "The jungle girl locked up in a casino with an erratic billionaire who has her own army?"

"Yes, Awen. A billionaire sent an army to catch that jungle girl. Seems whatever she knows is important."

"Oh, sure," said Emma, with an incredulous snort. "We're just going to march in there and get her, are we?"

Alex's wet eyes sparkled as he looked over at Fisch and Ludwig. "That's exactly what we will do."

CHAPTER 15

LATIFF

Eleanor Latiff paced back and forth in front of the Proteus Pod, fingering the tiny pebble deep in her pocket. After what seemed like a lifetime of searching she had the Eye. The image of her son glowed in her mind.

"Will it work?" asked Latiff in a calm voice.

"Yes," answered Coby. "Maybe. It's not that simple. We have never tested the pod on such a large scale. It's hard to say what will happen or—"

"Dr. Coby," said Latiff, her voice soft. "Is unlocking the secrets of magic for the betterment of all mankind not a noble goal?"

"Well, yes, of cour—"

"And have I not provided you with every imaginable resource?"

"Yes, but—"

"No," said Latiff, taking hold of Coby's lab coat. "No buts. Tomorrow night you will have more than enough energy to unlock that Eye. Because tomorrow night will change the course of humanity."

Straightening Coby's lab coat, Latiff smiled. "Besides, that boy, the Maskelynes' son, he activated the Eye without a fancy laboratory, did he not?"

Coby smoothed out his coat for himself. "That is hearsay. There's no empirical data to prove that."

Latiff tilted her head. "What if you had the opportunity to find out for sure?" She turned to face Captain Blaine, who had just entered the room, thrusting Savachia before him. Her face darkened. "Where is the Maskelyne boy?"

"He escaped with his sister," said Captain Blaine, giving Savachia a shake. "Thanks to this one."

Savachia scanned the room. He whistled. "Wow! Quite the place you got here. Whatcha making, cough syrup?"

Latiff took a deep breath and let it out slowly. "Where is the outpost?" she demanded.

Savachia shrugged. "Couldn't tell ya if I wanted to, sweets," he said. "And besides, I don't want to."

Latiff stood in front of Savachia. With a cruel smile, she brushed his hair away from his eyes. "My, my, have we made friends? Let me explain something to you, only because you remind me of myself, years ago. People like us don't have friends. When you have one singular goal, friends are a liability. Now give Captain Blaine the location or we will have to reconsider your mother's treatments."

Savachia didn't answer her.

Latiff crossed the lab to open a door tucked in the far corner of the lab. Captain Blaine pushed Savachia through the entryway after her.

In the middle of the room was a bed. Savachia barely recognized the woman in it. He wanted to believe it was the lighting and the faint glow from all the medical equipment that washed her of all color. He knew the truth. In a world of deception, cons and double crosses, one thing was certain: his mother was dying.

He had known it ever since his last visit to the Flatworld, the visit when he'd first met Latiff.

"You said you'd cure her," Savachia said, turning and glowering at Latiff. "If I helped you out, you said you'd make sure that she got better."

"But you haven't helped me yet, have you, hmmm?" Latiff asked.

Savachia dragged the locket that he always wore off over his head. He thrust the trinket at Latiff.

"Here, take it. I did what you asked."

Latiff pried open the locket, exposing the microcircuitry inside. Savachia knew that the locket had transmitted every word spoken between himself, Emma, and Alex on their quest to figure out the secret of the Eye.

"But you haven't yet done the final thing I asked." Latiff clutched the locket and stepped closer. "You were supposed to lead Emma and Alex Maskelyne to me."

Savachia shook his head. "They're my friends," he argued meekly.

"Friends." Latiff snickered. "You have a strange definition of that word. Spend the next few hours with your mother and consider where your loyalties lie. And then tell me what I need to know. After that, you will have many more hours to spend with her."

She turned to the other person in the room. "And, Captain Blaine, this is your last chance. Take as many soldiers as you need. Take the whole army. I only care that the boy makes it here alive."

The two left, snapping the door shut behind them.

Savachia watched his mother's eyes flutter open. She squeezed his hand.

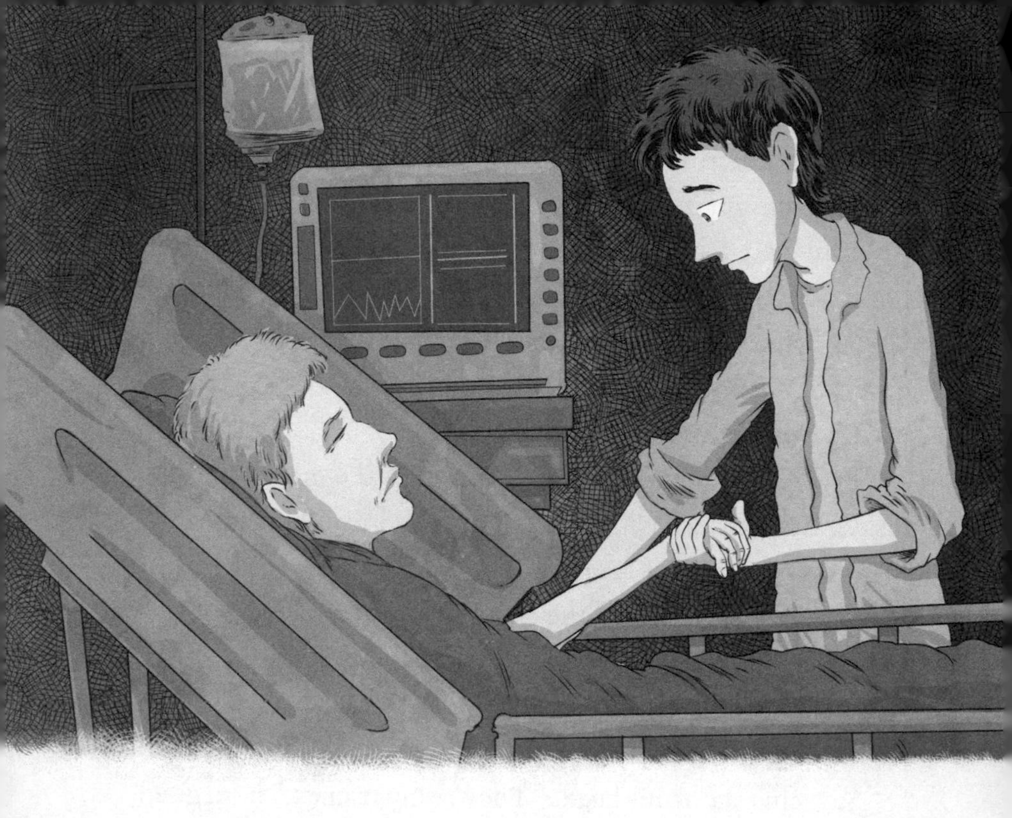

"My dear little Savachia," said Rachel. "What's to be done?"

"Don't worry about it, Mom," said Savachia. "It'll be fine."

"Fine?" said Rachel. "You sound like your father. Don't give in to that woman. She's willing to steal millions of souls to restore one. What makes you think she won't steal yours?"

"Because there's nothing left to steal," said Savachia.

CHAPTER 16

ALEX

"We can't just storm the Ka Casino!" Emma sat cross-armed on the couch in the atrium.

"We absolutely can." Alex leaned over the back of the sofa. "Please, Raisha, read the book again. We need any clue we can find before we take on Latiff. Think about it. We know Latiff wants the Eye, and she went to great lengths to capture Awen. So it has to be true that Awen knows a lot about the Eye." He threw himself into the back of the couch, and a small cloud of dust that smelled like damp concrete circled his head. "There should be another sign! There's a way, but we need something that tells us what we need to do!"

Emma's breath caught. "I think I know what the sign is," she said.

"What?" Alex gripped her hand. Then he noticed the tense look on his sister's face. Relaxing his hold, he leaned forward and said much more softly, "What is it, Em?"

Emma looked briefly to Fisch. He nodded. She locked her gaze on her brother. "Alex, I have psychic powers."

There was a moment of silence before Alex broke into a roar of laughter. He waited for everyone else to join him.

Nobody did. Emma just sat there, disturbingly calm. "You're serious?" he asked.

"I had a vision, Alex," said Emma. "I saw that woman's dead aunt back at Mr. Electric's casino, and then I saw Mom and Dad." She took a shaky breath. "Alex, they're . . . they're dead. Maybe they made it to Blackstone and—well, you heard what Raisha said. Or maybe they never even got there. I don't know. But I know we're not going to find them."

Alex looked from Fisch to Raisha to Ludwig for any hint of a joke. He found none.

"I, for one, think this calls for a round of tea," said Ludwig. "Raisha, I could use your help."

Gently, Raisha handed the book to Alex before following Ludwig to the kitchen. Alex looked at the old text for a moment and then dropped it on the coffee table. "Emma, what are you talking about? What do you even mean?"

"I mean," said Emma, "we aren't searching for our parents anymore. I mean you were right. This quest has always been about unlocking the secrets of the Eye. Or stopping other people from getting those secrets—people like Latiff. But we can't do that without a plan."

Usually Alex would spend a good five minutes gloating whenever Emma had to admit he was right. But suddenly he didn't want to be right, not this time. "Emma, I don't get it. You think Mom and Dad are dead? Because of a vision?"

Emma shrugged. "Magic is real, Alex. We both know that now. And you think fate's real. So why not visions?"

Alex shook his head. That kind of made sense, he had to admit. But Mom and Dad . . . dead? Alex left the couch, wandering around the room, not looking at anything in particular.

Soon, Ludwig and Raisha returned and served up steaming cups of tea. Alex barely noticed them. He was frantically turning the pieces of this puzzle round and round in his head.

Exactly what was Latiff up to? She knew Angel Xavier. He'd bet she was the one behind the Shadow Conjurer's technology, the machinery that drained magic from magicians to unlock the Eye.

But Angel Xavier was a magician. It made sense that he'd

want to use the power of the Eye to take control of the Conjurian. Latiff? She wasn't a magician, not that anyone had said. Why did the Eye matter so much to her? Why did she want it so badly that she'd kidnapped Awen, snatched Savachia, and lured hundreds of magicians to their deaths in some strange psychic challenge, trying to find someone who could truly contact the dead?

The dead . . .

"Her son!" Alex shouted, hopping onto the coffee table.

Raisha, hissing, managed to save the teapot from Alex's shoe.

"For the love of Dedi!" snapped Ludwig, wiping spilled tea from his lap. "What got into you?"

"Latiff's been running that psychic challenge since her son died, right?" continued Alex, ignoring the complaints. "The one with the ten-million-dollar prize?"

"Yes," said Fisch. "Would you kindly remove your foot from my spoon?"

"Right!" said Alex, stepping over to the couch. "She was looking for someone who could contact the dead."

"I suppose," said Ludwig. "Mainly we believed she was searching for candidates for her experiments. Magicians with real powers."

"But why just psychics?" questioned Alex. "Two birds, one stone, that's why. She'd get people to drain power from. And maybe she'd get somebody who could contact her son at the same time!"

"But then," interjected Emma, "if she keeps draining power from magicians, real ones, she'd lose the only way to talk to her son."

Alex shook his head triumphantly. "Not if she was going to do what Dedi had refused to. Remember why Dedi had to flee from Egypt in the first place? Why he ended up in the Conjurian? The Pharaoh wanted him to bring his wife back from the dead! And Dedi said no, but Latiff—"

It took a couple of breaths before everyone present realized exactly what Alex meant.

"She's going to bring her son back to life," Emma whispered.

Alex nodded. "But she'll need power. A lot of power. She'll need a lot of people to drain. Like the audience for a huge magic show."

Emma shivered. "Dedi refused because it was too dangerous, right?" she asked.

Arching over Alex, Raisha retrieved the ancient text

resting on the couch. She flipped through until she found what she was looking for. "This passage," said Raisha. "I didn't think it was important earlier."

"What does it say?" Alex leaned in.

"The veil cannot be lifted." Raisha traced the strange symbols with her claw. "The veil protects the great secret: death. Those who know the secret are gone. If they return and whisper the secret to the living, it shall bring about the great unraveling, a time of dark magic and endless suffering."

There was silence, except for the tinkling of Fisch's teacup as he unsteadily replaced it on the saucer.

"So if Latiff actually unlocks the Eye and brings her son back from the dead," Alex said slowly, "it means . . . the end of the world?"

"The Unraveling," murmured Ludwig. "My grandfather mentioned that once. I thought it was a myth like Armageddon or Ragnarok."

"We're about to find out," said Fisch.

"Not if we stop her," said Alex.

"How?" asked Emma. "The show is tomorrow night, and the city is already filling with people. Even if we got through the crowds, Latiff has an army."

"What if we had an army too?" asked Alex. Emma's frown vaporized his enthusiasm. "C'mon, you've done it before. One of us could go back to Conjurian City and get Derren to help us. If enough people—"

"No, Alex," said Emma softly, thinking back to all those people who had blindly rushed the Tree of Dedi behind her. The self-doubt rose in her like a tidal wave. She couldn't ask anyone to risk their life like that again. And besides, there was another problem with his idea. "There's not enough time to convince a ton of people to come to the Flatworld and fight some rich doctor and her minions."

"So we quit?" said Alex. "Just leave Awen in there? And Savachia too? And let Latiff do whatever she wants?"

Emma grimaced.

"Isn't quitting what you've wanted to do this entire time?" Alex demanded. "On the carriage, on the island?"

Alex saw how deeply his words bit into Emma. She lashed back. "I never *said* we should quit! I just said we need a plan! Why don't you ask fate, huh? Isn't fate supposed to be 'showing us the way'? Where's our next sign, Alex?"

Ludwig coughed. "It's late. Tired brains will do us no good. I propose a short siesta. We'll rise early and tackle this over a warm breakfast. Fisch's pancakes are much better than his card tricks."

Raisha rounded up several of Fisch's old capes to use as blankets and showed the kids and Pimawa into a small room next to the kitchen. None of them spoke another word. Sleep

came fast but not without nightmares of the dead returning for the end of the world.

EMMA

Gasping, Emma sat up in her makeshift bed. She could still make out the fading image of her parents against the dark. They'd come to her in her dreams . . . but they wouldn't be coming back in real life. They were gone for good.

Her brother and Pim were still asleep, draped in vibrant capes with bushy fur collars. Emma felt emptiness wash over her. Just hunger, she told herself. No, that wasn't it. She'd worked so hard, and Alex had too—to stop the Shadow Conjurer, to figure out the Eye, to find their parents. Now her parents were never to be found, they had no real clue about the Eye, and someone even worse than the Shadow Conjurer was about the destroy the world.

Why had they even tried so hard? What was the point? She wished Alex were right about fate guiding them. Then she'd have somewhere to place her hope. Her stomach gurgled. Okay, she was hungry too.

Sweeping aside her own checkered print cloak, she felt her way out of the dark room and around the corner. A row of figures, waiting and watching in the shadows, startled her until she realized they were only mannequins wearing costumes.

Unable to find the kitchen light switch, she edged along the counter to the fridge, removed the carafe of orange juice, and went fumbling for a glass in the cabinets. The sweet juice had just passed her lips when she saw green eyes watching her.

"Raisha?" she asked.

Then a second set of green eyes appeared, and a third.

She spat the juice and let the glass fall, shattering on the floor. Before she could yell, an electric shock ran through her. She dropped. Her body convulsed. She felt cold juice and glass shards against one cheek.

"That's the girl," said a voice. "She doesn't matter. We need the boy."

A roar tore through the kitchen. Screams and the crackle of electricity filled the room. Someone pulled Emma up, an arm wrapped around her waist. She tried resisting, but her muscles would do nothing but tremble.

"Are you okay?" came Fisch's voice in her ear.

"They're after Alex," Emma managed. Fisch dragged her toward the atrium as she slowly regained control of her legs. Something large and furry brushed up against her—this time it was truly Raisha, in her white tiger form. As they stepped into the atrium, Pimawa and Alex stumbled into them.

"Em, you all right?" said Alex.

"What's going on?" asked Pimawa, ears twitching.

"It's Sanctum," Emma gasped. "They've come for Alex."

"Why Alex?" asked Pimawa.

"How did they find us?" asked Alex.

"No time for that now." Ludwig rolled out of the shadows. "There's more coming."

Footsteps echoed from the elevator on the other side of the atrium. "Fisch," said Ludwig, "get them into the spirit cabinet!"

Fisch handed Emma off to Pimawa. He swung Ludwig around next to the kids. "You get them in there. I'll take care of Sanctum."

"No!" Ludwig said. "There's too many of them, you'll never—"

"Lud, we've been cooped up in here forever," said Fisch. "Doing nothing while these kids saved the Conjurian. It's our turn."

The white tiger chuffed, arching her back next to Fisch. "No, sweetie," said Fisch. "You have to go with them. You're the last line of defense if I don't . . . keep them safe."

Ludwig reached for Fisch's arm, revealing a tiny box covered in buttons in his hand. "Is that . . . ?"

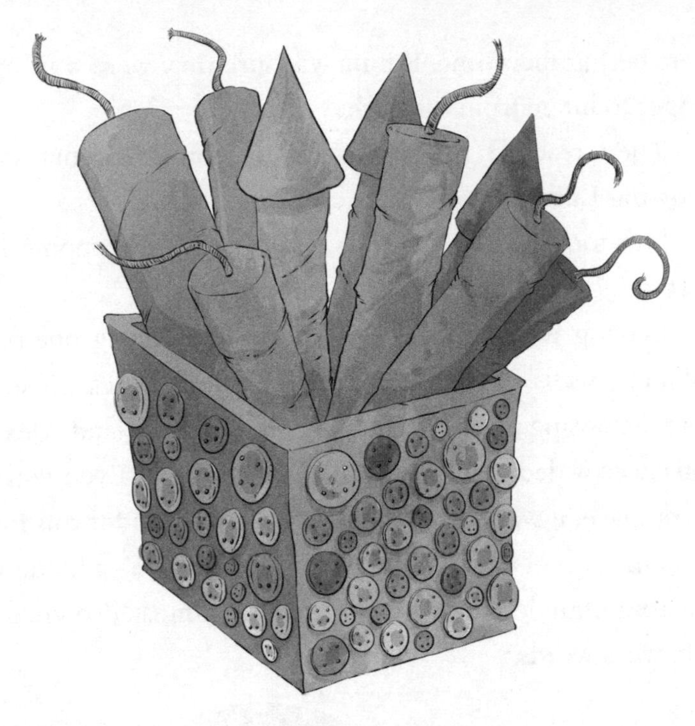

"Yes," said Fisch. "A few last pyrotechnics from our Fourth of July show. I set it up a few years ago." His smile shone in the darkness. "No goodbyes. Get moving. It's showtime!"

Ludwig spun his chair away from Fisch. "Be careful!"

"Of course," whispered Fisch from the shadows. "I'm the great and fabulous Fischbacher."

Ludwig took Emma from Pimawa, seating her on his lap. "Quickly! To the cabinet!" Even in the dim light, Emma caught the glistening tears on Ludwig's cheek.

The chair zigged through mannequins and zagged around the memorabilia crowding the floor. Even in the pitch-black, Ludwig knew his way. Behind them, Emma could hear cautious footsteps and muffled voices. The Sanctum soldiers were taking their time. Emma was sure they were waiting for a tiger to lunge from the dark.

They reached the old wooden cabinet. Emma stood, allowing Ludwig to open the creaking doors.

"It's too small for all of us," said Pimawa, hopping from foot to foot, anxiously watching behind them.

Ludwig reached inside and ran a hand along one of the cabinet's walls. Something clicked, and the back panel slid open, exposing a cubicle. Ludwig rolled inside, and Alex and Raisha crowded after him. Pimawa held back. Even with the extra space, it was clear the cabinet wasn't built for this many.

The flash of a firework illuminated Pimawa's silhouette as the roar thundered down the hall. It almost drowned out Pimawa's words.

"I'll stay."

Alex's eyes widened as he processed Pimawa's words. "No! We can't lose you again." Emma wanted to yell the same thing, but her throat felt clenched, her voice vanished.

Ludwig held the children back. Solemnly, he nodded to the Jimjarian. Before Emma or Alex could cry out again in protest, Ludwig pulled another lever, and the panel slid shut. A dull red light illuminated the tiny space.

Once more sitting on Ludwig's lap, Emma struggled to keep herself together. Her heart pounded, making her tremble. The last time she'd been in a space this small, she'd been buried alive in the dungeons that lay under the ruins of the Tree of Dedi.

Suddenly the room vibrated. Dust rose into the air. Raisha arched her back. Ludwig reached out to grip her broad shoulders. The giant cat shrank, returning to her two-legged form. More booms and the screech of twisting iron echoed from outside the cabinet.

The red light flickered. Alex grabbed Emma's arm. Raisha held Ludwig's hand. Barely audible over the noise, Ludwig repeated, "It'll be fine. It's all going to be okay."

Except Emma knew that wasn't true. She had survived being buried alive in the prison only to emerge and witness horrible devastation. She was sure this was going to be the same thing all over again, if they even got out.

CHAPTER 17

EMMA

When the door of the spirit cabinet opened, Emma stared out at a sight of destruction that made Latiff's plans seem inconsequential. It looked like the end of the world had already come.

Half the atrium's dome had collapsed, filling the space with tumbled rocks, twisted steel beams, and sparking electrical wires. The air choked them with dust and the taste of sulfur. She listened for any sounds of life but heard none.

Ludwig managed to get his chair out of the cabinet and struggled to roll it around the destruction. The wheels caught first on a piece of protruding rebar and then on a pair of mannequin legs that jutted out from under a support beam. Raisha helped, pushing him over to a circuit panel on the wall.

Ludwig opened the door and pulled a large switch. Floodlights around the perimeter of the cave flickered to life.

The effect was surreal. The swirling dust, like a dry fog, was penetrated by beams of yellow light.

"Fisch!" Ludwig's voice bounced off the mound of rubble.

"Pimawa!" cried Emma. She clambered onto a hill of rock, trying to get a look at the other side.

"Careful!" warned Ludwig.

Alex joined his sister, checking around and in between the stone and metal. Raisha assisted in the search. All of them continued calling for Pimawa and Fisch, their voices growing more desperate with every cry.

Raisha sniffed and clawed at the rubble. She zeroed in on a spot, reaching between metal girders, only to withdraw a single, dust-covered zebra-striped slipper. Tears dampened her furry cheeks as she brought the slipper to Ludwig. She collapsed next to his chair, the wild flare in her eyes smoked out.

Alex and Emma climbed down from the pile.

"I don't see any sign of them," said Emma. "Maybe the Sanctum goons took them." It was unfathomable to *hope* that their friends had been taken prisoner. But the alternative was . . .

Ludwig held the slipper up. The children dropped to sit by Ludwig's feet, coughing and wiping the wet dirt from their eyes.

Emma tried to think of something to say. She knew words would be of no help. If only she had made Alex stop this unwinnable quest and return to Conjurian City. Then they'd still have Pim.

But she hadn't done that. She'd followed Alex even when she knew he wasn't thinking straight. And now her parents were gone. Savachia had been captured. And Pimawa was . . . he was . . .

"I lied," said Alex.

"What?" said Emma, barely lifting her head.

"Before," continued Alex. "I lied that I wanted to find Mom and Dad and not just the secrets to the Eye. It's not that I didn't care about them, it's just that, well, you knew them. I've only known a world without them." He turned his head, avoiding Emma's gaze. "I knew you wanted to find them, Em, and so I said I'd try. But honestly, I was always thinking about the Eye. After I activated it, I felt something bigger than us, something guiding us. Even though I never had any parents, it felt like I finally had someone watching over me."

There was only one thing Emma could think to do at that moment. Only one thing she wanted to do. She wrapped her arm around her brother. "You do have someone watching over you."

"I always thought I'd find an answer to everything in books, in science. And then I thought fate would take me

where I needed to go." Alex pressed his face into her shoulder. "But now I've got no idea what comes next. What do we do, Em?"

For the first time since the Tower fell, Emma felt as if she knew the answer to that question.

Squeezing her brother tight, she said, "We stop Latiff. That's what we do now."

For most of her life, Emma had thought that her parents would come back and find her. They would keep her safe and tell her what to do. Wasn't that what parents were for after all?

Then she'd faced the Shadow Conjuror and nearly died. Nearly gotten everyone who trusted her killed. That had almost been enough to keep her from trying anything again.

But to her surprise, Emma found that old fear dissolving within her.

Her parents were not going to come back and protect her and Alex. *Nobody* was going to protect her and Alex. And Emma wasn't going to be able to keep everyone safe either. She might try. She might fail. She might let people down. She might let them get hurt—even killed.

Oh, Pimawa, Emma thought. *I'm so sorry.*

Because she was finally realizing that there was no magic in the world so great that it could keep the people you loved safe forever. That was an illusion, just like Pepper's ghost.

Emma knew that she wasn't safe. Alex wasn't safe. The world wasn't safe.

But that didn't mean she shouldn't try to save it.

"How?" asked Alex. "Stop Latiff how?"

Emma held him at arm's length. "I was hoping you'd have a plan."

ALEX

Over Emma's shoulder, Alex saw Ludwig and Raisha watching them. They had all lost someone in this last attack. And if they did nothing now, they'd lose each other.

For a moment, Alex thought he knew how Latiff must have felt after her son died. Alex would have done anything to get Pimawa and Fisch back. Just like Latiff had been willing to do anything to hug her son again.

"I know that look," said Emma. "What're you thinking?"

Thoughts drifted around Alex's brain like pieces of spiderweb floating in a breeze. He shook his head. A fine haze of dust rose from his hair as he tried to snatch up the pieces and make one coherent web.

"To the telescope!" he shouted as he stumbled to his feet, running wild up the tunnel to the observatory.

By the time Ludwig, Raisha, and Emma caught up to Alex, he already had his eye to the viewfinder as his fingers furiously adjusted the knobs.

"We don't have a lot of time," said Ludwig, brushing the dust from his watch. "If we're going to do something, we must get cracking soon."

"The show is tonight," said Emma, rising up on her toes to peer out the window. "What do you see?"

What Alex saw caused a cold sweat all over his body. He adjusted the telescope, scanning the crowd. The streets were jammed. "I've never seen so many people. There's no way we'll be able to reach the casino." He twisted another knob and focused in on the roof. He saw the same metal structure as before, except that now a tall cabinet sat on top.

"Can this thing zoom in any more?" asked Alex.

Ludwig rolled forward, pushing Alex's hands out of the way. As he made adjustments, Alex's face paled.

"I think I see Latiff!" said Alex. "There's a woman, anyway, and she's ordering everybody around."

"That'd be her," Fisch said, nodding.

"There's about twenty guards around her and a bunch of guys in lab coats. She's climbing up that pyramid thing to the box on the top. There's somebody with her. Can't see his face. He's putting something in the box, something small. I can't make it out. Like a pebble or something. Like the . . ."

Alex shot back from the eyepiece as if it was electrified. "The Eye. She has the Eye!"

"What?" said Emma, leaping forward to take a turn at the telescope. "That's not possible. You left it with Derren. I can't even see it."

"You don't have to see it," said Alex. "Just look at the whole setup. It's the same thing that the Shadow Conjurer was doing, just more advanced. She's going to try to unlock the Eye the same way Xavier did. She'll use it to bring her son back from the dead."

Emma stepped away from the telescope and shook her head. "She needs magicians for that, doesn't she? Don't tell me she's captured enough magicians to activate the Eye with her fake ten-million-dollar prize."

"Probably not," Alex agreed. "But what if—" He watched as all those people crowded around the casino, and his heart sank to his sneakers. "What if she's developed a way to drain power from everybody? Not just magicians? *Everybody?*"

"That's diabolical," said Emma. She bent to peer through the telescope again. "And that's—Alex, that's Savachia! The guy next to Latiff—it's Savachia!"

"Are you sure?" Alex bounded forward as Emma fell back. He pressed his eye to the eyepiece. "Oh, yeah. You're sure."

Latiff was talking to Savachia. He was answering her. He wasn't in handcuffs or closely guarded. He didn't look like a prisoner at all. He just looked as if he were helping Latiff . . . because he wanted to.

Alex lifted his head and looked at his sister.

"Your friend?" Ludwig asked.

Emma looked to Alex like she might explode from pure rage. "*Not* our friend. He was never really our friend."

Alex's stomach felt heavy and cold. "You think he was—Emma, was he working for *her*? For Latiff? All this time?"

Emma groaned. "I bet he was. How could we be so stupid?"

"Okay, okay." Alex felt as if his thoughts were stampeding away from him. He tried to grab at them, slowing them down. "We don't have time for this. We just have to assume Latiff knows everything we know. But it doesn't explain how she got her hands on the Eye. Derren had that. It was supposed to be safe. . . ." Alex rubbed his head hard with both hands until his hair stood up in all directions. Concentrate. Concentrate. He just had to think.

Emma eyed him. "Do you have a plan yet?"

Alex's thoughts spun and then suddenly clicked in like gears meshing with other gears, clockwork tickin on time. "Yeah, I do. Thanks to Mom and Dad!" He t to Ludwig and Raisha. "We need your help. We're goi the casino."

Ludwig looked at the boy. "That's not possible, my frien You saw for yourself. It would take us days to get through tha crowd, not to mention the army waiting for us at the door."

"Don't worry about that," said Alex. "An army has never stopped Emma before." He took a deep breath. "I'd say we need to do this for Pimawa and Fisch, but the truth is, we just have to do it, no matter the odds. I learned that from my sister."

Raisha placed her soft hand in Ludwig's. There was a faint green sparkle in her eyes. With a deep breath, Ludwig said, "We are at your disposal."

"Right!" said Alex. "Right." The thought of what was ahead made him woozy. "First, we need to salvage a few things from here." He headed down the tunnel back toward the atrium.

"Wait! What's your plan?" Emma shouted after him.

"Trust me," Alex replied. "It's a lot less terrifying if you don't know."

CHAPTER 18

ALEX

The air outside the outpost was thankfully cooler. None of them spoke a word as they left, tossing several large duffel bags into the van. Alex clutched the straps of his backpack as if his life depended on it. He looked at his sister, relieved to find that she looked just as nervous as he did.

They drove away from the outpost. The mound of rubble was now a graveyard, Alex thought. And all he could do for Fisch and Pimawa was to make sure they hadn't died for nothing.

The van rattled down the mountain in a storm of dust. At the main road, the van turned away from the strip and headed out of town. It was an easy ride to their destination.

Alex wished the rest of their trip would be as simple. Not a chance.

Ludwig guided the van off the side of the road, jerking to a stop between heavy underbrush and a chain-link fence. With Raisha at their side, they weren't worried about the dogs guarding the junkyard. Ludwig snipped through the fence with a pair of wire cutters. Emma and Alex led the way through the towers of junk, which provided much appreciated shade. Raisha pushed Ludwig's wheelchair, picking her way around ancient stoves and doorless refrigerators and the shells of broken-down cars.

They arrived at the giant clown's head, which was not a terribly reassuring sight in the light of the setting sun.

"You ready?" Alex asked Ludwig and Raisha.

They both nodded, and Alex could see the barely controlled fury in Raisha's tensed muscles. He so wished she were coming with him and Em.

"As much as anyone can be for this thing," said Ludwig, double-checking the rolled-up paper tucked in his shirt.

They'd spent the last several hours preparing. Ludwig and Raisha had scrounged up everything Alex needed. And while Alex put the finishing touches on the equipment, Ludwig changed into what he thought would be appropriate clothing—a khaki outfit with a jaunty safari hat.

In fact, it was a costume from his old jungle illusion, in which he played a hunter tracking down a savage lion—only it had been Ludwig who ended up in a cage at the end. That had all been fake. This was real.

Seeing the doubt on Ludwig's face, Alex said, "I know I

don't believe in fate guiding us anymore. But I still don't think it was blind luck that we met. Only you two could do this." Alex pointed to Ludwig's shirt. "Just follow that map and you'll be fine."

"It's not us I'm worried about," said Ludwig. "You two. I don't even know where to start."

"Then don't," said Alex with a smile. "We'll be fine. This isn't the first time Em and I have worked together to take down a monster on the verge of destroying the world. Should go a lot smoother than the last time, right, Em?"

Behind him, Emma was staring up at the clown's gaping mouth. It looked to Alex like her brain was awash in all the endless ways this might go wrong. "Hey, Em!" He got her attention, and she turned to him and tried to smile.

"We should get moving," said Raisha, adjusting the three large duffel bags on her back. "A lot to do and little time to do it in."

"She's right," said Ludwig. "We have to move."

Before he had finished speaking, Raisha hoisted him over her shoulder and scaled the tower of junk toward the gaping clown mouth.

"Good luck," Ludwig shouted, looking down over the duffel bags on Raisha's back.

"Can't rely on that anymore," said Alex to himself as he waved goodbye. The Wograth and the illusionist disappeared into the clown's mouth. A pulse of blue light lit up the clown's teeth a moment later.

"All right, Emma, our turn."

His sister had borrowed a stagehand uniform that Ludwig and Fisch had kept in their collection. It was all black, except for the muted gray LUDWIG AND FISCHBACHER logo on the back. But Alex knew she didn't feel ready. Emma shifted her feet in the dirt.

"I don't know, Alex," Emma said in almost a whisper. "This isn't going to work."

"Em," Alex told her. "I'm terrified too."

"What happens to us if we fail?" asked Emma.

"We die," said Alex. He'd been hoping for a light swat to the head, but he got no reaction. "I'm kidding. Look, Em, see those spotlights? That's the top of the Ka Casino. Whether we go or not, whether we die or not, that woman will try to open the veil between the living and the dead. The smartest person I know once told me that sometimes you have to stand up and fight. She was right."

Breathing deep, Alex pulled himself up the junk heap toward the clown head. He smiled when he heard his sister clattering up beneath him.

Once they were both inside the clown's mouth, they took a moment and stared out at the purple sky and the slash of orange that was all that remained of the setting sun. The spotlights from the Ka Casino crisscrossed overhead.

"X marks the spot," said Alex. "Ready?"

Taking his hand, Emma locked eyes with her brother. "Let's do it."

Hands clasped tightly, they stepped into the gateway together.

Alex had traveled through a gateway twice before, once leaving Uncle Mordo's and then departing the island. Both times there had been another gateway on the other side. This time there was only the hope of one. That was it. No cosmic force guiding him or keeping him and Emma safe. This either worked or . . . or he didn't know what.

The blue light splashed over his body, twisting and pulling it like taffy. He imagined it was like taking a bath with really weak electric eels. Then the light whooshed away, replaced by dry desert air tugging at his hair.

Alex took a second to get his bearings. Looking down, he saw that his legs were dangling in midair. Below he could see swarms of people. A burning sensation in his right arm made him look up. He was hanging on to his sister's ankle.

Emma was using both hands to grip a narrow catwalk that ran along the edge of the Ka Casino's roof. If she let go, they would both slide down the side of the casino to their deaths.

"Pull us up, Em!" said Alex.

"What do you think I'm doing?" his sister grunted back.

He closed his eyes, feeling every jerk as Emma struggled to hoist herself onto the walkway above her head. He felt himself rise several inches and looked up to see that Emma was now sprawled on her stomach on the platform, Alex's hand

still clamped around her ankle, his weight threatening to pull her back down.

She hooked one elbow around a railing and thrust an arm down toward Alex. "Grab my hand!"

Alex swung his other arm up, missing his sister's fingertips. His hand around her ankle slipped, and he heard her gasp.

"Come on!" she hissed at him.

He swung the arm up again, reaching, stretching as high up as he could . . . and the hand around Emma's ankle slipped off.

Alex waited for the rushing air, but it never came. Before he could fall, Emma's fingers clamped around his wrist, hard enough to bruise. She hauled him onto the catwalk with her, and they both lay flat for a second, catching their breath, locking eyes and not daring to look down.

"I think the fall would have blown our cover," Alex whispered after a minute or two.

Emma smiled weakly.

Alex sat up and cautiously looked around. Their catwalk ran around the entire roof of the casino. Clustered around the middle of the roof were dark-garbed Sanctum soldiers and scientists in white lab coats, their attention on the tower of scaffolding that had been built in the middle of the roof, the one with the pod capsule on its apex.

Emma gestured at a nearby outcropping of large metal tubes and whirring machinery, part of the casino's air-conditioning system, Alex figured. Alex gave a thumbs-up. They were too exposed here; any of the Sanctum people could see them just by turning around.

The two siblings made it to their cover and paused again to breathe. Carefully they peered around the edge of a generator. A few feet from their hiding place stood a row of Sanctum soldiers. Emma gasped, and Alex gripped her arm tightly. Two of the soldiers were holding a man with his hands cuffed in front of him—Derren Fallow!

"She captured Derren!" Alex whispered. "That's how she got the Eye!"

Emma's eye widened. "We'll rescue him," she whispered back.

Alex nodded. First the world, then Derren. Right. No pressure.

He looked past Derren at the woman in a white lab coat who must be Latiff. She stood in front of the framework that held the pod capsule. Tubes cascaded down from the pod, extending out to the four corners of the roof.

Alex had seen a similar setup inside the Tree of Dedi. There, the Shadow Conjurer, Angel Xavier, had used those tubes to siphon the magic from hundreds of captured magicians into himself, hoping to activate the Eye. This was a refined version of that tech—probably better, more powerful, more effective.

Alex followed the trail of tubes with his eyes and saw that they ran all the way down the side of the glass pyramid to the ground below, where thousands of people had gathered, waiting for the astonishing magic show that they'd been promised.

"She's going to do it," Alex whispered. "She'll use all those people to unlock the Eye!"

Latiff's voice boomed across the roof. "Turn it on, Coby!"

A thin man in a lab coat fussed with some switches. The pod hummed and shimmied in its iron nest. Bright light streamed down the tubes, cascading over the side of the casino. A white glow spread along the casino walls and out over the crowd, like the tide breaking on a sandy beach.

Alex glanced at Emma. She met his eyes, horror-struck, as the white light spread. Then a wave of blue light streamed back up the sides of the casino, directly into the pod, which channeled the power right into the Eye of Dedi.

A strange, unearthly moan drifted up from the people far below. The colors of the crowd seemed to fade—no, it was worse than that. The *people* seemed to fade. The blue light left an ever-growing sea of greenish ghosts in its wake.

Alex had thought the Rag-O-Rocs were the worst horror he could have witnessed. This was worse, far worse. Those people were being—not killed—*erased*. Was Latiff going to drain the entire city?

A numbing, sickly sensation gurgled in his belly. If they failed . . . all those people . . . He tried to shake off the stomach-churning thought. This was no time to throw up! Then he felt a gentle tap on his shoulder and looked at his sister's face. Her eyes sparkled, cold and focused.

"Now or never," Emma breathed. Crouching low, helping herself along with her hands, she crept across the roof, away from Latiff and the rest of the Sanctum workers.

Alex slung his backpack as quietly as he could on the ground in front of him and assembled his gear. He counted to thirty as he did so, for that was how long they had estimated it would take Emma to get into position.

". . . twenty-nine, thirty," Alex said softly. He pushed the button on the box he had set up at his feet. This had better work!

He remembered what Ludwig had told him when Alex revealed his plan. *The hand is not faster than the eye*, Ludwig had said. *It's all about audience management. Controlling what your audience sees and when they see it.*

As a steady stream of water vapor spouted from the box, Alex hoped he was right. This was the misdirection of the century. Hopefully, it would give Emma enough time to pull off the *vanish* of the century without getting caught.

CHAPTER 19

EMMA

Twenty-five seconds was all it took for Emma to reach the opposite side of the roof. The iron framework holding the pod was between her and Latiff. Luckily, Latiff had turned to face the rest of the Sanctum employees, which meant that her back was to Emma, and all eyes except hers were glued on the boss.

Actually, Emma noticed, there was one other person who wasn't watching Latiff. That traitor, Savachia, stood eyeing the heavily armed Sanctum guards. But why should that matter to Emma? Never again would she care what Savachia did or said or thought.

The blue waves of light crested up through the pipes and the pod, surging into the pod and then into the Eye. Latiff scanned the night sky above the casino and seemed to be watching for something. Only the crossing beams of the spotlights illuminated the dark.

"More power!" yelled Latiff. "Increase the range!"

"How far?" asked the man in the lab coat.

"The entire city! The state! The whole world if we need it!" said Latiff. "Keep going until—" She turned her head, still scanning the sky, and gasped.

Three feet above the roof, a ghostly phantom flickered to life.

"Jonathan?" Latiff's face softened. The hard lines melted. The tall woman faltered, gripping a nearby guard for support. "Jonathan, it's you! It worked. My son!"

Tears rolled down her cheeks. She remained rooted, mesmerized by the vision. "Come through, Jonathan!" she whis-

pered. "You can do it if you try. You have to come all the way back into the land of the living." She stretched out an arm toward the vision of her son.

Savachia, the soldiers, the scientists in their lab coats—everyone was staring slack-jawed at the apparition. Emma was close enough to hear Derren mutter, "She did it. She actually did it. She conquered death! It's not possible." And here it was: Emma's moment. She would not freeze, she told herself. She would not chicken out. "Here goes nothing, or everything," she said under her breath, and she jumped up onto the iron framework that held the pod.

It was like swarming up a jungle gym at a school playground—except that she'd never been as terrified as she was now. With every eye on the ghost of Latiff's son, no one seemed to notice Emma as she climbed. Now she was level with the pod, and the Eye of Dedi was within reach.

Blue light swam around the tiny pebble. No visible brackets held the Eye in place. Easy-peasy! Emma's hand reached out. Blue snaked around her fingers, and she froze.

The last time Emma had encountered this kind of power, she'd ended up a Rag-O-Roc and almost killed her own brother. And this blue light was filled with—what? A hundred times more power? A million times more? She'd bet that the weird pod had sucked the life from everyone within five miles of the casino.

An electric tickle ran up Emma's arm. For a moment, she was back in the Shadow Conjurer's grasp, her body spasming, joints popping as she transformed into a Rag-O-Roc.

But she shook off the memory. Maybe this would work, maybe it wouldn't . . . but she had to try. She'd take a page from her brother; she'd trust fate.

Emma clamped her hand around the tiny rock. Blue tendrils spiraled up her arm, licking her face. Her hair stood on end. She pulled.

The Eye didn't budge a millimeter. She yanked harder. Blue light engulfed her, and she felt her strength begin to drain. She would end up another soulless husk like the people so far below.

I tried, Mom. I tried, Dad, Emma thought. She clung to the Eye, but her arms sagged, her knees buckled, and her head fell back. She had failed.

ALEX

Alex crouched behind the generator, peeking out at Latiff, still mesmerized by his illusion. Pepper's Ghost. *Gotta love the classics,* he thought. Across the roof, he could see Emma start to climb up the framework that led to the pod. He felt a surge of pride. She was the bravest person he knew. And now she had her hand on the Eye.

What was happening? It looked like Emma couldn't pull the Eye free. No. They couldn't lose now because a stupid pebble got stuck! Alex's gaze swung back to the hologram. He was pretty proud of it, actually. With some help from Ludwig, they'd been able to replace Raisha's image with a picture of Jonathan Latiff from some old news footage. He'd thought for sure it would be convincing enough to give Emma time to snag the Eye.

But he hadn't counted on the Eye being so hard to snag.

That's when he heard a faint *FFFFSP* noise come from the small black box that was powering the projector. Oh no! The box sparked before a small cloud of smoke puffed out the back. Jonathan Latiff's image fizzled and vanished.

Latiff snapped out of her trance, confused. "What is going on? Coby! We had the veil open! I saw Jonathan!" Her eyes drifted up to the pod, and now Latiff did not seem confused at all. *"You!"* she snarled.

Emma was slumped against the pod, still clinging to the Eye. Latiff marched toward her. Time to improvise! Alex darted out from behind the generator, hoping Ludwig would show any second. They needed a little more misdirection.

Darting through the dazed guards, Alex was halfway up the scaffolding when a hand jerked him backward. And that was the moment the pod doors burst open with an ear-shattering boom.

EMMA

Emma heard a voice. A woman's voice. Maybe Latiff's?

"You!" said the voice. "You've done it!"

Emma's eyelids cracked enough to see Latiff standing below her. Weird, she didn't look mad. She looked happy. Emma could see tear marks on her cheeks.

Blue light poured from the door of the pod, and a sea of voices echoed together, ringing senselessly in Emma's ears.

"You did it," Latiff repeated, her voice full of awe. "You opened the veil!"

Latiff's face glowed with giddiness, but cold horror seized Emma. This was worse than being turned into a Rag-O-Roc. If what that old book had said was true, opening the veil meant the end of the world. And it was all her fault.

A familiar voice shouted, "Rip it out! Rip the Eye out, Emma!"

Alex? Her brother was on the ground with—huh, who would've guessed? Savachia had both his arms wrapped protectively around the younger boy. Ugh, Emma's head ached.

Her brain thrummed against her skull, making it hard to think. Then more voices:

"We're here, Emma! We're coming!"

That voice was vaguely familiar too. Whatever had happened when she grabbed the Eye must have scrambled her brain. That was the only way to explain the hallucination she saw now.

The pod's door creaked open, and two people peered out. Emma knew she must be having another vision, like the one at Mr. Electric's theater. Yet both the people inside the pod looked so real. The door between the living and the dead had been opened, and her parents were the first ones through. It was a lot to process right before the world ended.

Her hand slipped from the Eye. "I'm so tired, Mom," Emma whispered. She toppled back.

Arms wrapped around her, tight. "I'm here now, sweetie. I'm here," a soft voice murmured in her ear.

Emma opened her eyes. "Mom? Dad?" She was on the ground in front of the framework that held the pod, cradled in her mother's arms. Her father smiled down at her. They looked so happy to see her . . . but Emma knew she had to explain. To tell them the truth.

"I . . . I failed," she said. "I opened the door between the living and the dead. The world's going to end now."

"Hush, baby. Everything's fine." Evelynne Maskelyne rocked her daughter.

Her father petted her hair. "We're never going away again," said Henry.

ALEX

"Dad? Mom?" Alex stared at the scene before him. These were people he only recognized from photos. And yet, somewhere deep inside, he knew them better than anyone ever.

"Come here, Son," said Henry. "Look at you! Just look at you!"

Savachia didn't resist as Alex broke away from his hold. Alex watched, as if in a dream, as his father approached and knelt before him. The two strong hands on his shoulders were real. His father smelled of pine and dirt.

"I don't understand," Alex said.

"You don't have to, Son." Henry pulled him close. "There's a lot to tell you. Just not right now."

Alex pushed back. "But the Eye. The veil is open!" Over his father's shoulder, he could see Latiff still staring eagerly at the pod. Probably waiting for the real Jonathan to show up, but Alex had more important things on his mind at the moment. "And, well, we were trying to rescue Awen to find you. We were going to find Blackstone, learn how the Eye works. Emma had a vision. You were dead. You left the clues for me to find the Eye, but—"

Henry's laugh boomed. "Yes, of course you found the clues. But didn't you figure out the rest of it? That pebble is worthless. It has no power at all."

Alex stared. "No power? What are you talking about?"

"We wanted anyone who followed us to *think* that we'd found the true Eye of Dedi," Henry explained. "Then they'd waste their time searching for a harmless pebble and leave the two of you in peace."

"But I activated it!" Alex exclaimed. "It saved Emma."

Henry and Evelynne exchanged stunned looks. "You what?"

"WHERE IS MY SON?" Latiff's voice boomed.

Nothing had come through the pod after Henry and Evelynne Maskelyne, and Latiff had apparently gotten tired of waiting. She yanked a baton from a guard's belt and thrust it at Emma. "Tell me!" she bellowed.

Henry pushed himself between them, only to receive the buzzing end of the wand in his gut. He collapsed, and Latiff yanked Emma out of Evelynne's arms. She held the girl by one shoulder with the wand an inch from her throat. "You'll tell me where my son is or this will be a painfully short family reunion!"

"Let her go!" Evelynne jumped to her feet. "We have no idea what you're talking about!"

Tossing the wand aside, Latiff yanked a cord from the bottom of the Proteus Pod. She held it over Emma's chest. "Tell me where my son is!" Blue light swept over Emma. Her mouth stretched open in a silent scream.

"Stop! Stop it!" yelled Evelynne.

Henry swung his elbow into a guard's jaw and lunged toward Latiff. "You're mad! This is—" A second guard grabbed him and shoved him hard enough to send him sprawling.

Blinded by rage and the seething blue light, Latiff never even looked toward the shape leaping at her.

Savachia slammed into Latiff from the side. She buckled, releasing Emma as she fell with the boy on top of her. Latiff's teeth clenched with fury, and Alex winced as she wrapped one arm around Savachia's head and jammed the cord into his throat.

Alex gasped in horror as Savachia struggled with the little strength he had left, then went limp. Latiff held the cord in place until, suddenly, her arms passed through what remained of Savachia and her hands met the rooftop. Savachia's ghostly husk now hovered a few feet off the ground.

"Now tell me how to get my son back!" Latiff aimed the cord at Emma. Evelynne Maskelyne sprang to her daughter's side and wrapped protective arms around her. Emma's eyes fluttered open.

"If Jonathan doesn't get to be among the living, neither do you!" Latiff went on.

"He doesn't get to be among the living." Derren walked calmly forward, tossing his handcuffs to the ground and shrugging off the guards who had restrained him. "But stay away from the girl. I may have need of her later."

"What are you playing at?" Latiff's voice was coated with angry spittle. "Guards! Get him away from here now! Captain Blaine!" No one responded. "What are you clods doing? Grab him!"

The guards lined up behind Captain Blaine, who stared menacingly at Latiff.

"Captain Blaine, if you would," said Derren.

Captain Blaine nodded. The guards swarmed Latiff.

CHAPTER 20

ALEX

"Derren!" said Henry, moving to greet his old friend as Alex stared, openmouthed. "So good to see you! I know you must be upset at us for hiding the truth and faking our deaths. We had—"

Derren sidestepped him, gazing up at the open portal inside the pod. "Well done, Emma. Well done."

Alex felt an uneasy puzzlement stir deep inside him. Derren didn't seem that surprised to see his two old friends back from the dead. And exactly what had he meant about maybe needing Emma later?

Just then Geller exploded out of one of the air vents near the generator, thrown off-kilter by the large rucksack clamped in his beak. He circled around the platform before landing on his master's shoulder. "Everything is ready," he told Derren. "Although I would not be against a quick meal before we head out."

"What's ready? What're you talking about?" Henry Maskelyne frowned.

Alex did too.

Derren grinned, and Alex felt chilly inside. What was there to be cheerful about, exactly, when Savachia and thousands of people in the street below had been turned into phantoms? When a gate had been opened between the living and the dead and the world was about to end?

Derren made a gesture at Captain Blaine, who left two of her guards to keep ahold of Latiff and headed over for a roof-

top door near the generator. She opened it, and two men inside dragged out a skinny girl with a tangle of blond hair—Awen!

Awen's hands had been tied in front of her, and the two soldiers held her tightly as they marched her over in front of Derren. They seemed far more fearful of her than Alex would have expected two armed grown men to be of a girl not much older than himself.

Derren beamed at Emma, ignoring the rest of them. "My dear girl. I could not be more proud. You and your brother found Awen before Latiff. Impressive! If the Grubians had reached the three of you before Latiff got to Awen, all this might have been avoided."

"What's Awen got to do with anything?" asked Alex, eyeing her. She snarled at Derren through a tangle of hair that hung over her face.

"Shall I tell him?" Derren nodded at Henry, then at Evelynne. His brow crinkled in mock puzzlement. "Oh, that's right. You didn't know I knew. So clever, using the buried-alive illusion to fake your deaths. Didn't think I would figure it out. But who came up with that trick again? Oh, yeah. *Me!*"

Derren reached into Geller's bag, withdrew gloves, and tugged them over his hands. "Don't look so confused," he told Henry. "It's not your fault, really. Good heavens, your kids had almost caught up to you." Derren smiled kindly at Alex and Emma. "I suppose, given how much you have done for me, I *could* tell you the oldest secret of magic. Would you like to know?"

Everyone stared at him. Alex had a feeling that he didn't want to know whatever Derren was about to say. But somehow all he could do was listen.

"Dedi didn't create the Conjurian. He stumbled into it," said Derren. "Heck, he didn't even do that much. *She* did." Derren pointed a gloved finger at Awen, who growled back. "Act your age, my dear," Derren told her. "She's the one who opened up the first portal from the Flatworld to the Conjurian, just to get her father away from the pharaoh who wanted his head."

"Hold on," Alex managed to say. "I mean, I knew Awen was way older than she looked—but you think she's Dedi's daughter?"

"My, someone *has* learned a lot on their little field trip." Derren chuckled. "You had almost all the pieces. But you never realized that the silly pebble you entrusted to me—I was so very touched, Alex, truly—was meaningless. Powerless. Just as your father told you. It is this little girl who is actually the Eye of Dedi."

"How do you know that?" Henry Maskelyne positioned himself between his family and his old friend. "We only learned that at the dig site. You weren't there. No one else knew. No one else was there to know."

"Yeah, not quite." Derren winked at Geller.

"Indeed," said Geller. "I must say, Master Maskelyne, you and your wife are a formidable team. Your planning after your discovery was fast and effective."

"Your bird was spying on us?" shouted Henry. "For how long? Why?"

"I was and will always be two moves ahead of you," said Derren. "As to why, that's not important anymore—to you, at least."

"You lied to me," Latiff snarled. She was glaring at the pod. "You told me that pebble had the secret to conquering death!"

"Ah!" Derren grinned at Latiff. "I didn't quite lie. It was . . . misdirection. No one could ever bring someone back from beyond the grave. Your son, my dear, is gone. But the Eye of Dedi does have another way to conquer death." His eyes were fixed on Awen now. "Don't you, darling?"

"So . . . the world's not going to end?" Emma said shakily, staring around her. "I thought if Latiff opened up a portal between the living and the dead . . ."

Derren laughed. "Is that what you thought would happen? How noble of you, to try to stop the Apocalypse. I'd expect nothing less of your children, Henry. But no. The world's fine. And I finally have everything I need—control over the Conjurian, Awen, and the Proteus Pod, which of course was never supposed to unlock a stupid little rock. It is, in fact, a highly evolved gateway. All I needed was a strong psychic connection to someone already in Blackstone—to Henry and Evelynne." He smiled at Emma. "You provided that, Emma. And now I've opened up a path to where I want to go."

"What?" Evelynne stared at Derren. "You did all this . . . you stole the souls of all these people . . . so you could get to Blackstone?"

"Of course I did." Derren's smile looked like a wolf baring

its teeth. "Because we both know what awaits me there, don't we? It is the heart of magic after all."

Evelynne shook her head. "No. You can't. No one's going anywhere." Evelynne jumped to her feet, moving Emma behind her.

"Oh?" Derren put his hands on his hips. "Are the king and queen of hide-and-seek going to stop me?"

"No," said Alex. "They are."

As Derren cocked his head quizzically at Alex, a glob of red jelly smacked his face. "What in the—"

Jelly rained down from the sky on Derren and the Sanctum guards.

Alex stared up and felt his mouth drop open. Even wilder than the jelly storm was the object hovering over the casino. The Grubians' carriage! A balloon with the gold-and-purple LUDWIG AND FISCHBACHER logo emblazoned on the side had replaced the mast. Gertie, once a mere quadruped, stood under the open mouth of the balloon. A jet flame roared from a compartment on her back.

"Ahoy!" responded Neil Grubian, who, with surprising grace, grabbed a rope and spun down along the side of the carriage. He pirouetted across the door and then grabbed the handle and swung it open, pinning himself behind it.

"Yes!" shouted Alex. He could see Ludwig and Clive inside the carriage, chucking jelly snowballs, careful not to hit their friends. Looking at Derren and Captain Blaine, he said, "Speaking of being two steps ahead, bet you didn't see this coming!"

Captain Blaine squinted at the odd ship. "See what coming?" she sneered at Alex. "Do you actually think they're going to chase us away with . . . ?"

Tasting the gloppy substance on his face, Derren said, "Jelly!" Quickly he used his vest to scrub the sticky sweet stuff from his face. Then he stripped off the vest and flung it away from him before scrambling up the iron framework and taking refuge under the Proteus Pod.

A strange chittering sound filled the air. Captain Blaine was the first to get hit. Her head snapped back as if smacked by a bowling ball. Her spiked red hair stretched in every direction. Small rips appeared in her uniform. She buckled over, swatting at invisible attackers.

The Sanctum soldiers, who all had jelly splattered on faces or clothes, had only a second of befuddlement before they too were convulsing, grabbing at things that they couldn't see but could definitely feel. Armed men swung their wands haphazardly, zapping each other.

Overhead, a ladder unfurled from the side of the balloon. Before the ropes could hit the roof below, Pimawa and Fisch were already climbing down while Neil and Clive continued the assault from above.

Awen took the distraction as an opportunity to elbow one of her captors in the gut. The other had let her go in order to slap himself in the face as something tried to pull his eyebrows off. Awen skittered away, rushing into the chaos.

"Retreat!" yelled Captain Blaine, clawing her way to the doorway that led back inside the building.

Henry and Evelynne snatched up their kids, shielding them as best they could, pressing close to the iron framework that held the Proteus Pod. "You brought imps?" exclaimed Henry.

"Yeah," said Emma, grinning. "They really love jelly."

The Sanctum guards followed Captain Blaine to the stairs, struggling to seal the door. After it closed, their screams echoed from the stairwell. The rooftop was quiet, except for a few remaining imps licking up a spot or two of jelly. Alex and Emma bolted for Pimawa, nearly hugging him unconscious.

"We thought you were . . . ," wept Emma.

"Best trick ever!" said Alex. "Ha! And Ludwig thought his greatest magic was behind him!"

Clive Grubian, still clinging to the side of the carriage, shook the rope ladder until it clattered on the roof. "Last call for Conjurian City," he shouted. "All aboard!"

"The Grubian brothers?" Evelynne Maskelyne said doubtfully.

"They're our friends," Alex told her.

“And, as the heads of M.A.G.E., your new bosses,” Neil added. “And I order you all to get up here tout de suite! Those imps won’t keep Sanctum at bay forever.”

“We can’t go,” said Emma. “We’re not done here. All those people and . . .” Her eyes wandered over to the ghostly image of Savachia.

“Never mind that rat,” said Alex. “What do we do with *him*?” His face twisted with disappointment and anger as he pointed at Derren, still huddled beneath the pod.

With a savage yell, Awen charged from behind the generator. She slammed into the iron scaffolding and shook it hard, smiling at the fear in Derren’s eyes.

“We’ll deal with him later.” Henry Maskelyne started to climb up to the Proteus Pod. “First, we have to shut this down!”

“Can’t that wait?” asked Emma.

“No, no, it can’t,” said Evelynne.

“Er, why? What is on the other side?” asked Fisch, nervously pulling his cape around him.

The answer came in the form of an arrow, swishing out of the portal. It sliced through the rope ladder.

CHAPTER 21

EMMA

Emma stared in horror as at least twenty Wograths armed with multi-bladed spears and bows exploded from the pod and leaped down onto the roof. Jabbing their spears, the Wograths herded everyone into a group. Henry and Evelynne grabbed the kids. Pimawa snarled as menacingly as he could, despite his shaking ears.

One of the Wograths prodded Derren out from under the Proteus Pod. The tallest warrior, her face plastered with red paint, stepped toward Awen.

Awen, however, was not hiding. With a feral growl she leaped at the Wograth, slashing with her nails. Two of the long-eared warriors aided their leader in subduing her, pushing her down next to Alex.

The red-faced Wograth clanged her spear on the iron platform. "Henry and Evelynne not stay here. Must return to Blackstone." Her English was broken, but her intentions were not. She leveled her spear at Awen. "You return to Blackstone." Then she leveled her spear at everyone present. "You all go to Blackstone. Know too much."

"Mom, Dad, what's happening?" Emma clung to her mother.

"Garria!" Henry Maskelyne pushed the Wograth's spear aside. "Evelynne and I will return, but the others stay here."

Garria shook her head, prodding Henry with the spear. "No."

Henry looked at Awen. "Garria, we will go with you. Let Awen stay. These people can take care of her."

"No." Garria didn't change her expression. "She go."

"Why?" Emma grabbed at her mother's arm. "Mom, what are they doing? Why do they want us to go to that place?"

Evelynne, worried, looked down into her daughter's face. "They see themselves as the guardians of the Conjurian. Of magic itself. They don't want anyone who knows too much about Blackstone out in the world—and that includes us. And Awen. And now you."

"But why?"

Evelynne's eyes rested on Derren. "Because of what some might do with that knowledge."

Emma shook her head. Then she straightened up, glaring at Garria.

"You can't just order people around," she said fiercely. "I don't care if you think you're the guardian of magic or not! Anyway, I opened that portal, and I don't know *anything* about magic. Other people are going to do it too. People like them!" Emma pointed at Latiff and Derren. "You can't just hide away and take us with you and expect that to work."

Alex scrambled forward, standing next to his sister. "She's right. People are always going to figure stuff out. We're good at that."

Garria regarded Latiff and Derren suspiciously. Then she circled Emma and Alex. "You opened the portal?"

"Yes," said Emma. "I wasn't even trying to. But if you let us stay here . . ." She nodded. Garria was listening to her. They were all listening. She just needed to keep talking. "Or in Conjurian City, maybe. If you come with us to Conjurian City, you can teach us about what Blackstone really is. You can teach all the people, and the Jimjarians, too. We can help each other, instead of fighting each other. Because . . ." She tried to remember something, something Derren had said. He had called Blackstone *the heart of magic*. Emma wasn't sure what that meant, exactly . . . but the memory seemed to make the right words flow into her mind. "You're the guardians of magic, but you're not the only ones. We've been trying to watch over the magical world too. Trying to help it. Trying to bring magic back to it." She took a deep breath. "We can help you. We can work together."

"Come with us," Alex added. "Come see Conjurian City. Shouldn't you at least know what it is you're protecting?"

Garria clanged her spear on the iron bars. The other Wograths closed in on the prisoners. She swung the spear in an arc less than an inch from Alex's and Emma's noses. Alex jumped back, grabbing at Emma to pull her with him.

The arc of the spear continued as Garria spun around and sliced through the cords connected to the Proteus Pod.

Deprived of its power, the portal within the pod swirled faster and faster, smaller and smaller, shrinking like a dying blue sun.

Henry sighed with relief and Evelynne put her hands to her face as Emma realized what had happened. Garria wasn't going to make *anyone* go back to Blackstone. Her speech had worked.

ALEX

Timing is everything to a good magician, Alex thought afterward. Derren knew just how to seize the right moment. He hooked his foot around the ankle of the Wograth next to him and swept his leg out from under him. Then he sprinted for the scaffolding. Reaching the top, he dove into the portal a millisecond before it winked out of existence.

Alex gaped. Emma gasped. "He got away!" shouted Fisch.

"I wouldn't call that getting away," said Evelynne with a shiver.

“He got what he wanted,” said Henry. “He’s in Blackstone now. Although he won’t like what’s waiting for him on the other side. Will he, Garria?”

The leader of the Wograths flashed her sharp teeth in a wicked smile. With a kinder smile, she looked at Emma. “We go with you, to Conjurian City.”

“We can’t leave all these people like this,” said Emma. She moved to the roof’s edge and gazed down at the ghostly crowd below.

“I don’t know what we can do for them,” said Pimawa, joining Emma at the roof’s edge.

Fisch squeezed Emma’s shoulder. “It’s not your fault, sweetie.”

“We might be able to reverse it.” Alex frowned, thinking it through.

“It can’t be reversed,” said a weak voice. It came from Latiff. She’d been flung to the ground when Captain Blaine’s soldiers had stampeded for the exit, and she sat up shakily now. “All that energy, or magic, whatever you want to call it, was used up. We never developed a way to reverse it.” She shook her head. “Then again, I could be wrong. I thought that portal would connect the worlds of the living and the dead, not this earth and some place called Blackstone. So far it seems I’ve been mistaken about everything.”

Emma crossed the rooftop to kneel down in front of Latiff. To Alex’s amazement, she almost looked as if she felt sorry for the woman.

“All this for nothing,” said Latiff. “Science was my life.

It was everything until it couldn't save Jonathan. Then I thought magic held the secret until a magician fooled me."

"There must be something," said Alex, joining them on the ground. He didn't have to like Latiff to try to get some information out of her. "Which of your scientists built it? Whoever did the work might know of a way to—"

Latiff's laugh was anything but joyful. "Such a sweet boy. You remind me of my son. Always believing the best in people. But Sanctum, all of it, was Derren's the entire time. None of them will do anything for me now."

"Come down this instant!" came Garria's angry voice from behind.

Alex and Emma spun around. Awen had climbed on top of the iron scaffolding supporting the Proteus Pod.

Awen shook her head. She frowned and then began to speak, haltingly at first but more clearly than Alex had ever heard her before.

"My father, he knew the pharaoh wanted my power. Everyone did. So he helped me escape. First from Egypt to the Conjurian. Then from Blackstone to my island. What good did that do?" Awen looked at Garria. "You think it's your duty to protect me. I understand. I see now what that has done. But I don't want to live in a cage forever."

"Forever?" Alex said. "She's really . . ."

"Immortal," Henry answered, looking at Awen sadly. "And she never wanted to be. We were going to come back from Blackstone to help her if we could . . . but the Wograths wouldn't let us leave."

"Awen?" said Emma. "What're you doing?"

Alex felt a cold little shiver inside him as Awen smiled from behind her dreadlocks. "You are correct too, Emma Maskelyne. Sometimes you do what is right, even if it means death. To live forever is not a curse. I was wrong. It's a gift, and one that I can share."

Her hands shot skyward. Brilliant white light pulsed out from her in expanding circles, moving down around the casino and out across the Vegas streets.

Alex and Emma raced to the edge of the rooftop and peered over, watching as the circles of white broke over the soulless crowds.

"She's doing it," said Alex, dazed. "She's bringing them back to life!" He lifted wide eyes to Awen. "She really is the strongest magician there's ever been!"

EMMA

Awen's waves of light rippled on, leaving living human beings in their wake. Soon the streets filled with the noise of confused and dazed Angel Xavier fans wondering what had happened to the show they'd been promised.

Emma spun around. Savachia stood behind her, looking unsteady on his feet. Head hung low, he did not look at her as he spoke.

"I'm sorry. I know you have no reason to believe me or ever trust me again. But she had my mom. I didn't know what to do." Tears welled in his eyes and ran down his cheeks.

Emma stared at him. Her fists balled up at her side. She was severely tempted to sock him in the nose.

But then his words sank in. He'd betrayed them . . . but he'd done it for his mother. That was something Emma could understand.

"Yeah, you did. But you know what else?" Emma said, and sniffled. "You saved me." Savachia's face lit up with shock as Emma threw her arms around him.

Alex turned away in embarrassment. "Ew, gross, Em." And then he yelled, "Awen!"

Emma jerked out of Savachia's embrace to see Alex scramble up the framework and catch Awen's lifeless body as she tumbled down from the pod.

"She's not breathing!" Alex shouted.

Emma raced to the platform and, with help from her mom and dad, lifted Awen down. Evelynne stretched Awen flat on her back, resting her head on her chest. "No heartbeat!"

"I thought she was immortal?" said Emma, gently shaking Awen's arm.

"She was," said Alex, and Emma realized for the first time what Awen had actually done.

"She gave her immortality up to save all those people," she whispered. "Life for life. Oh, can't we help her?"

Henry Maskelyne laced his fingers together and compressed Awen's chest again and again. "We promised we would cure you! Let's breathe, Awen! C'mon, sweetie!" He paused at regular intervals, allowing Evelynne to press her ear to Awen's lips.

But that wasn't the right thing to do, Emma realized. Awen hadn't had a heart attack. She'd given up the magic that had granted her eternal life—and so magic would be needed to cure her.

Emma reached for Alex's hand.

She had magic, didn't he? She'd had visions—real ones. And what about Alex? He'd changed Emma back from a Rag-O-Roc into a human girl. They'd all thought it was the Eye of Dedi that had done it, but their father had said the Eye was nothing but a pebble. So the magic must have come from Alex himself.

And what about her mom and dad? They were magicians too. They just needed to do what Awen had done—to give some of their magic away.

"Dad. Stop!" Emma grabbed at her father's hands. "That's not going to help her. We need to—"

Her father and mother seemed to understand at the same moment. Evelynne reached over to lay her own hand on Henry's. Now all four Maskelyne hands—Emma's, Alex's, Henry's, and Evelynne's—were suspended in midair above Awen's motionless chest.

"But how . . . ?" Henry breathed. "There's no spell for this. How can we give part of our magic to her?"

Emma closed her eyes. Somehow the answer was inside her.

"Just think of her. Visualize the power leaving our hands and entering her," she said softly.

A white glow surrounded their joined hands. "Oh my," Fisch said softly from behind them. "I do believe . . ."

The light reached out from the Maskelynes' hands to Awen's chest. It seemed to soak through her skin.

With a gasp, Awen opened her eyes.

Before she could do or say anything Emma wrapped her arms around her. "You're alive!" she cried out.

Confused, Awen looked at Henry and Evelynne.

"How do you feel?" asked Evelynne, laying a hand on Awen's forehead.

"I feel . . ." Awen's face softened. Her grimace melted into the tiniest of smiles. "I feel normal?"

Alex joined in on the hug. "You saved everyone!"

"Ugh! Off!" Awen pushed the kids away and gingerly got to her feet. Taking a deep breath, she patted her arms and legs. "I *am* normal," she murmured.

"Wait." Alex raised an eyebrow. "So you're not immortal anymore?"

"I think no!" said Awen with joy beaming from her face.

Henry and Evelynne pulled all three kids together and squeezed them hard. "We are so proud of you!" Evelynne reached out and pulled Pimawa close. "All of you!"

After the group hug relaxed, Alex asked, "What now?"

Henry chuckled. "Did you already have another adventure planned?"

"No, I mean," said Alex, "what about bringing magic back to the Conjurian? What happens if another villain tries to destroy the world?" He shot a quick look at Latiff. "No offense, but it's kinda true."

"What now, indeed." Henry Maskelyne clamped a hand on his son's shoulder. "I think for a good long while we should work on being a family."

"People willing to sacrifice themselves for others, that's true magic," said Evelynne. "And it's alive in everyone."

Wailing sirens rose in the night air. Suddenly all eyes were on Latiff.

"There are going to be lots of questions." Henry looked over at his wife.

"Best not to stick around, then," came Neil's voice from above.

The flame above Gertie's back was snuffed out, and the

EPILOGUE

"Geller!" shouted Derren. He propped himself up, wiping the slimy wetness from his eyes. "Geller, where are you?"

The sharp fern leaves sliced his hands as he felt around. "Ow!" Derren blinked, removing the rest of the mud from his eyes. Everything around him was dark and humid. Vegetation choked out the daylight—or maybe it was night? He had no idea.

"I am here, Master Derren." Geller tumbled, tail feathers over beak, out of the trees behind Derren. "As to where we are, I can only assume we made it to either Blackstone or the nearest sewage treatment plant." Geller groomed the muck from his wings.

Suddenly Derren didn't care about the damp humidity or the swampy ground. With renewed vigor, he plodded through the underbrush, ignoring the spiked and thorny plants biting at his legs and arms. "We are in Blackstone!"

Hopping from branch to branch, Geller stayed close behind. "Yes, we must be. Only 'we,' though, minus Awen."

"We don't need her." Derren trudged on with a sinister grin, a man on a mission.

"Ah," said Geller. "I was under the impression that you were going to steal her immortality. I really should invest in a notebook."

With a laugh, Derren abandoned all caution and broke for the needle of light ahead. "We don't need to steal anyone's immortality anymore. We'll have our own. Don't you understand? We are in *Blackstone*, Geller!"

"Yes," said Geller, now flying from tree to tree. "You did mention that."

"We don't need her, or Xavier, or Latiff, or any of them." Derren stumbled every several feet. Pure obsession kept him moving, crawling and pulling his way through the jungle. "I don't need any of them. This is Blackstone! Death cannot find me here!"

The dark canopy gave way, opening onto a cliff overlooking a valley. The sun blazed in the purple-and-yellow sky. Derren skidded to a halt inches from the precipice, gawking in wonder at the scene spread out below.

The valley stretched for miles, fading into a hazy mountain range in the distance. Between the cliff and the mountains was a sight that Derren was almost certain no magician since Dedi or his daughter had laid eyes on. A row of enormous pyramids stretched into the horizon. Each was larger than the next, built from a rock that morphed colors in the light. Purples, blues, and greens swirled on the sides of the hulking structures.

"Praise Dedi," said Geller, wiping his glasses on his feathers.

"Forget Dedi," said Derren. "We are at the heart of the Conjurian! Every secret of magic lies in that valley. Each one is mine!"

"Fantastic, sir." Geller peered over the edge before flapping nervously backward. "Do we admire those secrets from afar, or do you know of a way down?"

Skipping wildly in a circle, stones plummeting off the cliff, Derren grabbed Geller's wings and swung him around. "A small, insignificant worry, my dear Geller! It doesn't matter if

it takes us ten years to get down there! We have all the time in the world!"

"Oh, marvelous." Geller wobbled. "Perhaps then we will have time to order a pizza and some breadsticks."

A faint rustling interrupted the celebration. Both Derren and Geller turned toward the jungle. A line of Wograths emerged, with more and more appearing behind them. Spears leveled, they marched forward.

"A welcoming committee," Derren said to a trembling Geller. "I'm sure they know the way down." Derren opened his arms, a showman's smile on his face. "Greetings, my friends! I am Master Derren Fallow, and this"—he gestured toward the parrot hiding behind his legs—"is my colleague, Geller."

The Wograths continued their slow march, forming a half circle around Derren and Geller. The tallest warrior stepped forward, sniffing the air, then growling low and deep.

"And you are?" asked Derren.

"Tresssspasssser," said the Wograth.

"Well." Derren raised his eyebrows, quickly smirking down at Geller. "That's an interesting name. Perhaps you could—"

"No tresssspassers." The Wograth raised his hand. The line of warriors resumed their march, pushing Derren and Geller toward the cliff edge.

"Hold on a minute!" Derren looked over his shoulders. Three inches of ground left. "I am Derren Fallow, ruler of Conjurian City! I have come to—"

The spear tips pressed into Derren's chest, piercing his shirt.

"You should have stayed in your city," the Wograth snarled. "Trespassers aren't welcome here." The Wograth gave his spear a nudge, and Derren's heel slipped over the cliff edge. Geller squawked, soaring off over the valley.

"Geller!" shouted Derren, grasping the spear shaft. "Geller, come back! I need you—" He grimaced as the spear's point pricked his skin. His mouth opened to protest. He managed only a shrill yelp as he fell off the cliff.

ACKNOWLEDGMENTS

I want to thank my wife, Tammy, and my son, Liam, for always being there and putting up with my long hours.

Thank you to my agent, Rosemary Stimola, who always believed in the magic even when I didn't. And to Allison and everyone at the ever-expanding family at Stimola Literary Studio, thank you for the infinity pool of support.

Thank you to Phoebe Yeh, my editor and guide through the most daring illusion of my career. And to Elizabeth Stranahan, April Ward, Melinda Ackell, and Sarah Thomson, my eternal gratitude for piecing together this entire Las Vegas magic show.

About the Author

Brian Anderson is the author of several children's books, including the Conjurers trilogy (*Rise of the Shadow, Hunt for the Lost,* and *Fight of the Fallen*) as well as the picture books *Nighty Night, Sleepy Sleeps; The Prince's New Pet;* and *Monster Chefs*. He is also an optioned screenwriter and the creator of the syndicated comic strip *Dog Eat Doug,* which enjoys an international fan base both online and off-line. Brian's uncle was a charter member of the Magic Castle and taught him his first card trick in second grade. He has been practicing magic ever since. Visit theconjurers.com to read the free Conjurers graphic novel today.